SHERLOCK HOLMES:

THE CENTURION PAPERS

THE SECOND COLLECTION

The Davies Brothers

thedaviesbros.com
Twitter and Facebook: @thedaviesbros
Instagram: the_davies_brothers
GNP Press

Copyright © 2019 The Davies Brothers.

All rights reserved. No part of this publication may be reproduced, distributed, or transmitted in any form or by any means, including photocopying, recording, or other electronic or mechanical methods, without the prior written permission of the authors, except in the case of brief quotations embodied in critical reviews and certain other non-commercial uses permitted by copyright law.

Any references to historical events, real people, or real places are used fictitiously.

Front cover artwork and design by Rhys Aneurin.
www.rhysaneurin.com

First printing 2019.

GNP Press
United Kingdom & Japan

Dr Watson's *Centurion Papers*
A Note from the Editors

It would be unusual to find anyone born over the past century and a half who is not in some way familiar with the adventures of Sherlock Holmes. We are no exceptions. Dr Watson's gripping accounts of his long-time companion's exploits thrilled us as children and continue to do so as adults. However, our interest in Holmes and Watson's stories was purely recreational until we were contacted – through a convoluted chain of friends and acquaintances – by a newsagent in Northamptonshire. Geraint James asked us to record for posterity his son's recent battle against the M League, the heinous secret society created by Professor Moriarty himself. You will, of course, be familiar with many of the events related to 'The Holmes List' through the countless news reports, as well as the litany of publications investigating the most shocking political scandal of our times, but our good fortune in obtaining first-hand testimony of the affair resulted in our comprehensive account, *Hudson James and the Baker Street Legacy*, gaining a certain renown among Holmes scholars and the public at large.

We were delighted to have made a small contribution to the canon of work devoted to the great detective and his wider circle of allies and foes, but we were each satisfied to return to our more mundane existences as lecturers and researchers, Nicholas in Wales and Brett in Japan. That was until, quite out of the blue, we received an email from Sarfraz Malik, Senior Vice President (Media Relations) for Letts International Banking Corporation. In his message, Mr Malik suggested that we may be able to assist his staff in curating the contents of a safety deposit box that had recently been opened in the Strand branch of LIBC. The box had been left in the bank's care exactly one hundred years ago (when it was known, simply, as Letts of London) under express instruction that the contents not be released until now. However, Mr Malik admitted that his colleagues were at a loss exactly what to do with the documents they had found inside: a thick packet of handwritten papers penned by its depositor, Dr John H. Watson.

Naturally, our curiosity was piqued, and we each made the journey to London – Nicholas from Cardiff; Brett from Tokyo (an airfare that has yet to be reimbursed) – so that we could examine this important historical discovery more closely. Our initial excitement was tempered somewhat upon seeing the physical condition of the papers. They had been tied together by string made of a coarse hemp, which had absorbed some of the Indian ink from the pages (this was presumably the work of a careless clerk rather than of Watson himself, who was famously fastidious in the preservation of his accounts). Additionally, there was evidence of damp inside the steel box, causing rust damage to transfer from the lining of the container and onto the papers themselves. LIBC's unceasingly helpful resident historian, Sandra Beardsley, explained that the supposedly impenetrable basement of the Strand branch had flooded in 1940 – a burst waterpipe resulting from Luftwaffe bombing during the Blitz.

We would eventually require the services of the British Museum to help separate the pages and restore those sections where the ink had smeared or disintegrated completely. Through a combination of state-of-the-art computer modelling techniques and MRI scans, as well as the diligence, skill and dedication of the museum's restoration unit, we were finally able to gain an almost complete set of documents from which to work. (Special thanks to Drs Andi Tilson and Desi Murty for their talent, good humour and endless supplies of instant coffee!)

It was almost six months after first receiving Mr Malik's initial email that we could, at long last, begin the task of reading John Watson's papers. Even after so much sterling restoration work, this was no easy procedure. There was the problem of Watson's spidery handwriting making some words difficult to decipher (he was a GP, after all). Then, while some stories betrayed elements of the distinctive prose style so beloved of millions (these accounts presumably intended for publication before Watson chose otherwise – or had that decision made for him), others were in mere note form. In a few of the cases, the reports were even written in code, so sensitive were the contents.

The curation and verification process has been helped in part by the covering notes that Watson attached to most of his reports. While these were not intended for publication, we have included them here due to their historical significance and in order to give some context to the events on which he was reporting. Dr Watson dated these notes, and it is interesting that he appeared to be planning for some time to compile this packet of stories for delayed publication. What we could not discover from any of his papers, however, was exactly *why* he chose to deposit the documents in the bank when he did. Holmes had long retired by this time (aside from a brief return at the beginning of the war), so it seemed unlikely that Watson was waiting to include any new adventures. It may be that following the initial successes of the German Spring Offensive on the Western Front in early 1918, Watson felt a greater urgency to ensure his legacy remained intact (which lends a certain irony to the fact that it was during the *next* World War that we nearly lost the entire collection to a German bombardment).

Holmes scholars will, of course, be aware of Watson's legendary army dispatch box, referred to at the beginning of *The Problem of Thor Bridge*, containing unpublished accounts of some of Holmes's cases. Those same scholars will know that, according to Watson's tale, the box was secured in the vaults of Cox and Co., at Charing Cross, and *not* at Letts on the Strand. In recent years, at least twelve different historians have claimed to have unearthed the same dispatch box and made the contents available for publication. We have no reason to doubt the integrity of any of these individuals, and we are sure they each released their findings in good faith; however, the very fact that Watson revealed the *precise location* of the box in print suggests that – to paraphrase his colleague – some game was afoot. As our recent investigations in Northamptonshire confirmed, Holmes and Watson were well aware of Moriarty's influence even after his death at Reichenbach, so the doctor's very public reference to this dispatch box was almost certainly a ruse designed to lead Moriarty's dark disciples in the wrong direction. While we concede that Watson may have left some reports of a more trivial nature in the care of Cox and Co., perhaps in the hope of persuading the M League that they were the very extent of Holmes's investigations, we are confident that our discovery is Watson's most important – and most shocking – legacy.

Throughout the arduous curation process, we have gained fresh admiration for the work of Watson's contemporary editor, Sir Arthur Conan Doyle, who perhaps deserves greater credit for fleshing out Watson's accounts with such verve and narrative flair. However, we must also remember that the sometimes shocking and ghastly contents of these newly-discovered stories may have rendered Watson's writing less cohesive than in some of his more famous adventures. We have attempted to emulate his (and Conan Doyle's) usual style in those reports left incomplete, while at all times striving to maintain the absolute truth of the events.

The Davies Brothers

The Missing Parrot

Covering Note to *The Missing Parrot*

Mr Sherlock Holmes often accused me of imbuing our adventures with rather more romance than necessary, and of favouring the sensational over the intellectual. I must admit that, among all those cases I committed to print, there was a bias toward the most thrilling and bizarre, but this is only because his public (and I am very aware that the readers of my little reminiscences were *his* public, not mine) demanded that.

Now, regrettably, having completed my final report on Holmes's death at the Reichenbach Falls, I have foregone any further contributions to *The Strand* in order to allow myself time to reflect upon this tragedy. While the country lost one of its most brilliant minds and justice its keenest investigator, I lost my dearest friend. As Mary told me in her infinite wisdom, 'The physician vows to heal all, and that includes the physician himself.'

However, as my mind's eye paints that scene above the waterfall afresh each night, and makes it ever more vivid, I find myself faced with empty hours of sleepless contemplation, and without recourse to my one refuge from the soul's dark musings. Once more, I am indebted to my dear Mary for urging me to write again, not for the public's sake, but for my own. The intuition of the fair sex is seldom wrong, and I confess to gleaning a certain excitement in finally recording some of these cases that I had previously neglected, even as I am aware that they may never be seen by any eyes but my own. The pen transports me from the gloom of my dimly-lit study and carries me back to the thrill of the hunt, when I was honoured to accompany my friend as he untangled yet another web of mystery. It is fanciful, I know, but in the rapture of composition I can almost sense that Sherlock Holmes is still with me and that one day, perhaps, we shall reunite for more adventures.

For now, alas, I shall content myself with my recollections of those mysteries that, for one reason or other, I failed to commit to paper sooner. One such of these is the case of Lady McMillan's missing parrot, in which my own actions brought me too much shame for me to lay bare to the public at large. Yet, it is a story so weird and unexpected that I feel compelled to record it and remember how the deductive talent of Mr Sherlock Holmes brought to justice one of the most cold-blooded criminals he ever encountered.

John H. Watson, M.D.
August 24th, 1891

I. Rodney's Disappearance

It was one of those glorious September afternoons in which the sun warmed London after a miserable weekend, allowing us a brief interlude of summer before the dark autumn months ahead. Mary and I sat in an amicable quiet at the large French windows that overlooked our modest back garden, reading novels and enjoying the vibrant colours of the flowers that we had nurtured so diligently over the preceding months. It may have been just one of many blissful afternoons in the company of my bride (for we had been married less than a year), if it were not for the unexpected but welcome interruption of Mr Sherlock Holmes.

I confess that since my bachelor days had ended, I had rather neglected my friend and my visits to Baker Street had become less frequent as the months passed. Yet I still read with keen interest the newspaper reports of his exploits, both at home and on the continent, and vowed to reacquaint myself with my companion of so many extraordinary adventures. Frankly, it had never occurred to me that Holmes would ever seek my counsel, so it was with some surprise that I welcomed him into my home.

'Watson, I am in need of your unique talents,' he said as he sipped his tea. I noticed Mary's smile of pride, and felt my cheeks redden at this compliment.

'Gladly, my old friend. Whatever is the problem?'

Holmes waved his hand casually. 'An obligation to Mycroft to assist one of his colleagues.'

Mary leaned forward. 'Your brother? An issue of national importance, then?'

'Nothing of the sort. A mere trifle, in fact, which is why I require your husband, if you would allow it.'

I tried to ignore the thinly veiled insult in his request. 'What is it, Holmes? I'd be only too glad to help if I am able.'

'Lady McMillan's parrot.'

'I beg your pardon?' I asked. 'A parrot?'

'Yes. She's terribly upset about it. It seems that the parrot was… abducted.'

I could not hide my amusement, and neither could my wife. I even sensed a flicker of mirth in Holmes's eyes.

'Why on earth are you investigating such a case, my dear fellow? Why, just last week you were assisting the king of Spain, were you not?'

'The prince,' Holmes sighed laconically.

'His missing crown,' Mary interjected. 'I read of it in the papers.'

'It was but a morning's work, my dear.' He lowered his voice conspiratorially. 'Approximately a third of my cases are the result of somebody imbibing too much wine, and another third the result of an illicit liaison.'

'Holmes!' I cried, concerned that my Mary would be offended by his frankness.

'Come, come, John,' she chastised gently. 'This is fascinating. The prince of Spain, Mr Holmes?'

'His misfortune was the result of *both* vices,' Holmes whispered with a raised eyebrow. 'Thankfully for His Royal Highness, I was able to trace the crown before any great scandal should occur.'

Mary almost squealed with delight, such was her amusement, and I was reminded once again of the tolerance and humour that had attracted me to her with such fervour on an otherwise dreadful evening two years prior.

'But what of this parrot?' I asked.

'Well, after Mycroft helped me so generously in that small matter of the Russian ambassador and his missing manor house…' I chuckled at the memory, and I could sense Mary's curiosity, but Holmes continued before she could interrogate him on the matter. 'I have been rather in his debt. Lady McMillan implored me to help her trace this bird and, as her husband is one of Mycroft's closest colleagues, I was compelled to acquiesce. But I fear that it will be a case requiring sensitivity rather than intellect, which is why I seek your assistance, Watson.'

Once again, I ignored the sharp edge to his words, simply pleased to be invited to join him on another case after some time, and, with Mary's blessing, I was soon on a train bound for Oxford. Looking back now, this was one of my happiest memories with my dear friend and I venture to claim that the great detective was as overjoyed to be back in my company as this humble doctor was to be in his. Holmes's recent adventures in the palaces and offices of some of the most exalted names in Europe had brought him notoriety and, no doubt, significant financial reward, but I perceived a tiredness in his eyes that hadn't been there when we shared lodgings, and I fancied that he may have been succumbing to exhaustion. On that warm Monday afternoon, however, I could sense his mood lightening as we shared a platter of sandwiches during our journey and talked amiably of our recent experiences. He was never more content, of course, than when embarking on a new investigation, and the case of Lady McMillan's missing parrot provided him with the intellectual stimulation without, I presumed at that time, the pressure of the goddess Justitia requiring swift and definitive results.

A pleasant cab ride to the outskirts of the old university town took us to the manicured estate of Lord and Lady McMillan, and we were greeted at the door by the man of the house. William McMillan was an impressive figure, with handsome whiskers, a sturdy frame and the ruddy, appealing complexion of the sportsman. I well knew that his athletic appearance belied a shrewd mind that, according to more than one newspaper, made him one of the prime minister's closest confidantes.

'Mr Holmes.' He spoke in a hushed, serious tone. 'And Dr Watson, I presume. I should be very glad if you could examine my dear lady wife. She is quite beside herself about Rodney.'

'Rodney?' I asked.

'Her parrot. Poor Marcia's sick with worry. She's barely eaten a thing, and I'm very concerned about her.'

'Of course,' I assured him as he led us up the ornate double staircase. 'When did you learn of Rodney's... disappearance?'

'Late last night.' It was a woman's voice, strong and shrill, but with an unmistakable quaver of sadness. We looked up to see a plump lady in a bright purple gown and dark veil. She gripped the first-floor banister as if unable to bare the weight of grief for very long.

'Marcia, my love,' Lord McMillan cried, 'you should be resting. You've had a dreadful shock, my dear.'

'These men are here to help us find Rodney,' Lady McMillan countered, 'so it behoves us to give them every assistance...' She signed plaintively. 'However trying that may be.'

McMillan looked concerned, but his wife let go of the intricately-carved banister, took a restorative breath, and walked slowly down the steps towards us. Her elegant dress swished behind her rhythmically, lending a regal frisson to the scene. As she approached, her husband went to her and lent his arm. She lifted her veil and smiled meekly from her heavily-powdered face.

The four of us walked through to the family room, and I was moved to gasp as I crossed the threshold. It was an incongruous sight inside this rural English manor. There were countless plants about the large room from all corners of the earth. Orchids and Venus fly traps, rubber plants and cacti, the gayest of flowers and the most malignant-looking vines. This cacophony of flora appeared to be consuming the room, dangling above the divan and armchairs, and even coiling around the leg of a coffee table. The odour was not unpleasant, the perfume of a hundred varieties of flower combining into an unclassifiable fragrance that reminded me somewhat of the Indian jungle. Holmes and I removed our jackets in the humid air, and Lord McMillan ordered the morose butler to bring us some cold squash. Holmes and I sat on armchairs either side of the divan, upon which the lord held his lady's hand soothingly.

'We returned from a weekend in town to find Rodney missing,' Lady McMillan said. 'I'm sure it was Annabel.' Her eyes darkened when she said the name. 'One of the maids.'

'Where is this Annabel now?' Holmes asked.

'Gone,' Lord McMillan said, before his wife could reply. 'She was new to us this June and barely competent, but I'm sure she is not capable of such a crime.'

'She was a wretched child, William,' spat Lady McMillan. 'You don't have to defend her now.'

'Well, she was not always diligent in her duties,' her husband said. 'I admit to using some strong words on her, as did my wife at times, and we were about to end her employment. But I'm sure she is not to blame.'

The lady snorted at this.

'You suspect that she took the parrot out of spite, Lady McMillan?' Holmes inquired.

The gentleman again answered the question ahead of his wife. 'Annabel was rather fond of Rodney,' he said. 'I cannot imagine that she would have hurt him.' I could not ascertain whether Lord McMillan's haste to reply was to protect his wife from further strain, or to prevent her from telling us all she knew.

'I see no other explanation,' the lady argued. 'William had given most of the staff the weekend off as we were in London. Only Annabel remained, along with Carruthers.'

'The butler,' her husband explained.

'He's a dear,' the lady continued. 'Been with us for twenty years. And he swears that he knows nothing of what occurred. He went to church yesterday morning. When he returned, he noticed that Rodney was...' The poor lady could not finish the sentence. 'I'm sorry, gentlemen. William said that I would be wasting your time.'

'No, dear,' her husband uttered without conviction.

'But I've read of your talents, Mr Holmes,' Lady McMillan sniffed. 'I knew that if anyone could find him...'

'It's possible that Rodney simply flew away,' her husband continued as he stroked the lady's hand tenderly. 'The latch on the cage is—'

'The cage was locked,' the lady piped up, her strength returning, 'but Rodney was no longer there. He could not close it himself! When Carruthers tried to find Annabel and ascertain what had occurred, he realised that she was gone too.'

'Her belongings?' Holmes asked.

'She did not possess a great deal,' replied Lord McMillan. 'A young girl, no more than eighteen years, so just a few clothes, I believe.'

'Did she take them with her?' my companion pressed.

'I... I'm afraid I do not know.'

'Mr Holmes,' the lady wailed imploringly, 'will you find my Rodney? And will you bring that girl to justice? I beg you!'

Sherlock Holmes has a penchant for insensitivity and an ill-hidden distrust of the fair sex; yet he was also possessed of a remarkable tenderness when the situation called. He rose from his chair, stepped towards the grieving woman and spoke gently but firmly. 'I assure you, my lady, that I will get to the bottom of this mystery.' His words soothed her nerves markedly, but before she could voice her gratitude, Holmes looked keenly around the strange room. 'Ah! I take it this was your parrot's home.'

He walked over to a golden cage suspended like a chandelier from the ceiling, quite large by the standards I was used to seeing in the parlours of friends and patients in London. The McMillans and I were silent spectators as the amateur detective examined the cage, until we were interrupted by the solemn Carruthers bringing our drinks.

'The very man!' said Holmes to the butler. 'It was you who discovered this disappearance, was it not?'

Almost imperceptibly, Carruthers' eyes flitted to his employer, and Lord McMillan nodded his assent. The thin, hawk-like, old man cleared his throat and spoke with the carefully rounded pronunciation of the experienced manservant.

'I came back from church at around noon.'

'How long had you been gone?'

'I left at half an hour after nine, for the ten o'clock service in the village. His Lordship is kind enough to allow me that time every Sunday.'

'So you followed your usual routine?'

'To the minute. I'm sure never to dawdle. When I returned, I was taken with how quiet it was. Usually Rodney would greet me.'

'Greet you?' Holmes looked surprised.

'Rodney was a very clever boy,' Lady McMillan said. '"Hallo!" he would call whenever he heard the front door open. And he would often make us laugh, wouldn't he, dear? Repeating little things we would say. He even learned our names. "Willie! Willie!" and "Marcey! Marcey!"' As she quoted the bird, she even mimicked its squawk and I'm ashamed to say that I had to hold a glass to my lips in order to hide my laughter. 'Such a clever boy…' She sniffed into a handkerchief, and Holmes ordered the butler to continue.

'Well, sir, I immediately came here to check, and I realised that Rodney had gone.'

'And the cage?' Holmes pressed. 'The door was closed?'

'It was closed tight. Locked. I called out to Annabel – she was the only person home – but received no reply. I searched high and low all afternoon and into the evening until the lord and lady came back from London, just before eight. But of Rodney and Annabel, nothing was to be seen.'

'And were there any other visitors while the lord and lady were away?'

'No, sir.'

'No deliveries, no callers of any kind?' Holmes was keen to press the point.

'I'm certain of it. It was just me and Annabel, until she took off.'

'Did you notice anything else unusual, anything out of place or missing?'

'Well, yes, sir. The Ercuis silverware–'

'The cutlery?' Lady McMillan asked in some alarm. 'William, did you know?'

'I did not want to worry you, my love,' her husband whispered. 'You already have so much with which to contend.'

'It was a wedding gift from my aunt,' the lady explained. 'A priceless collection, one of Ercuis's very first designs. That... vicious little girl!'

The butler continued. 'We kept it in the dining room. I noticed that the drawer in the cabinet was slightly open. When I looked inside, the entire set was gone.'

'Thank you, Carruthers,' Holmes said. 'That will be all.' With his master's nodded permission, the butler exited. My friend turned to the lord and lady and his tone was instantly sympathetic. 'And, may I ask, what was your business in London?'

'Just a weekend in town,' the lady said, 'before it becomes all too cold and foggy. We went shopping on Saturday, then I dined in our Mayfair apartments alone while William attended to some government business.'

'Matters of state do not always follow the conventions of society, unfortunately,' Lord McMillan chuckled. 'The prime minister required some assistance in a rather delicate matter regarding the Palace, so I was obliged to go to Downing Street.'

'William joined me again for lunch yesterday, and we enjoyed a matinee at the Lyceum, then tea, before returning home...' The lady fell into sobs once more.

'I would very much like to investigate this girl's quarters,' asserted Holmes.

William McMillan led us to the servants' wing and a door at the end of the corridor that was tucked beneath a staircase. Beyond this door was a small, gloomy room with no furniture but an iron-frame bed and a narrow chest of drawers. A thick, coarse lady's cloak hung on a bronze hook, and next to this was a faded photograph of a man in soldier's uniform, standing alongside a pretty young woman holding a baby. The picture was framed in a crude piece of folded card.

'As you see, she did not possess a great deal,' said Lord McMillan quietly. 'We thought that we were being charitable in giving her an opportunity. She had no references and little experience, but the agency insisted that she could be relied upon.'

As the gentleman spoke, Sherlock Holmes barely listened. He was on his knees, examining each drawer one-by-one. There were a few loose pieces of clothing, but otherwise they were empty.

'Curious indeed,' murmured Holmes as he stood. I must have rather blushed when I saw what he was holding in his fingers: a single black stocking made of an exquisitely delicate fabric with an intricate lace patterning at the band. Lord McMillan and I both coughed and looked about us in some bashfulness. It was typical of my friend, of course, that he did not concern himself with matters of propriety; instead he was concentrating solely on the puzzle that this undergarment posed him.

'Gentlemen,' he said in his matter-of-fact way, 'it is imperative that we find the companion to this piece.' With that, he fell to his knees again and searched the floor. The peer and I looked at each other with no little embarrassment, then we too joined the search for that most intimate of items.

In such a small room, it was quickly apparent that the other stocking was not to be found. Holmes stood and left the room, leaving Lord McMillan and I to follow, the master of the house showing no little irritation at his famous visitor's odd behaviour.

'Mr Holmes!' he called as we walked the corridor of the servants' wing. 'What, may I ask, is your line of inquiry here? You are my guest, yet you act as if—'

'A thousand apologies, my lord,' said Holmes. 'We shall not impose much longer, I fancy. Now, I would like to see the gardens. No, there's no need to accompany me; you neither, Watson. I require solitude and quiet, if you'd both be so accommodating.'

'But, but...' the politician blustered. 'What are you planning to do? What do I tell poor Marcia?'

'I regret to say that of Rodney's whereabouts I am unclear. However, at the very least I intend to bring his assailant to justice.' And with that, Holmes made for the front entrance and left us.

'Your friend,' McMillan muttered. 'Is he really as talented as we have been led to believe?'

'Certainly,' I told him, 'there is no finer mind in England.'

The lord stood still, as if struggling to comprehend my assurance, then he turned to me. 'It is becoming late. Would you care to join us for dinner, Dr Watson?'

It was a simple but hearty repast of ham, game soup, bread and vegetables. I had become accustomed to city life since my return from Afghanistan, but Mary had recently professed a desire to leave London for more bucolic surroundings. This delicious meal, which Lady McMillan boasted had been made entirely from homegrown ingredients and – in part, at least – prepared by her husband, certainly encouraged me to consider my darling's wish more deeply. I was heartened, too, to see the lady of the house regain some strength from the refreshment, even as her husband relayed his doubts over Holmes's ability to trace her beloved pet.

'No, no, no,' she insisted. 'You've told me, dear, how highly Mycroft speaks of him. He will find Rodney, I am certain.'

'I will do my best, madam.' We turned as one to see Sherlock Holmes returned from his hunt with mud stains on his trousers and sleeves. 'But I'm afraid we may be too late.'

Holmes's straight, serious expression seemed to pierce Lady McMillan's resolve and the colour drained from her cheeks. She emitted a terrible groan of despair and quickly swigged back a long glass of gin.

'Mr Holmes!' her husband snorted as he took her hand. 'Really, your behaviour has been quite trying. I beg you show some restraint.'

'We shall impose no further. Watson, I think we may be better served nearer home.'

'Now?' I asked between mouthfuls of ham. But the glint in Holmes's eye told me that he was in no humour to wait, and within the hour we were on the train back London. Before embarking, Holmes arranged for a wire to be sent and I overheard him tell the messenger the name of the recipient, 'Mr Mycroft Holmes.' Clearly, my friend was keeping his brother informed of our progress in a case that concerned his colleague.

If, on our ride to Oxford, Holmes had been unusually convivial, on this return journey he was again his taciturn, introspective self. Even after some time away from his company, I knew not to interrupt Holmes's thoughts, and I was content simply to serve as witness again to some knotted mystery that the consulting detective would soon unravel.

On arriving at Paddington, we hurried to the telegraph office, where Holmes received reply from Mycroft.

'Ahh, as I expected,' he murmured as he read the telegram.

'What is it?' I asked, unable to contain my excitement.

'We are in more treacherous waters than it first appeared, but…'

'But *what*, Holmes?'

'But patience will be our guide through these murky waters.' As galling as Holmes's aloofness could be, I knew that any further interrogation would prove futile. Like the conjuror at the end of a performance, Holmes would reveal his great *denouement* only when he was ready. 'Now, my dear Watson, you are a man of responsibility, and I advise you to return to your lady wife.'

'Holmes!' I protested.

'Do not fear, my faithful friend. I shall call upon you as soon as I receive further data. Until then, we are both in the same unhappy position… We must wait.'

I must admit that my patience was sorely tested. I had remained silent on the train, presuming that our adventure would continue upon arrival in London. I had not inquired about Holmes's search in the gardens of the McMillan estate; nor had I questioned him over his intended actions. But that was when I had imagined I would soon be privy to Holmes's findings. Instead, I endured a lonely hansom ride home through the muggy night, my mind filled with more mysteries than when I had departed that afternoon.

II. The Search for Annabel

The next few days must have been as trying for poor Mary as they were for me. I jumped every time we received a visitor, desperate for word from Holmes. When we talked, my mind wandered, and when we played cards, I was soundly beaten every time. It pains me to say that my melancholy was the cause of our first argument as husband and wife, Mary ordering me to stay home as she kept a dinner engagement at Dr and Mrs Farnsworth's residence alone.

It was on the fourth morning after my visit to Oxford that a messenger boy arrived at our house with a note. Mary sighed with relief when she saw the ludicrously simple missive:

Come at once. SH.

My dear wife already had my coat ready as I ran to the door. We embraced, all ill will forgotten, and I took the short cab journey to Baker Street.

After a brief reunion with Mrs Hudson in which she insisted that I had put on at least two stone since my wedding day, I joined Holmes in our old sitting room. How quickly we forget old routines, I mused, and how soon we remember them when we return to old haunts. It felt the most natural action to fall instinctively into my favourite old armchair and examine the same range of tattered volumes atop our – or should I say, *Holmes's* – cluttered bookcase. I felt an odd combination of joy at returning and sadness at the knowledge that never again would this place be my own. But as I looked about the habitually untidy room, I realised that it had never truly been mine, filled as it was with the papers and files as well as the scars of various scientific experiments, all belonging to my more celebrated friend. In fact, it looked no different now than it had when I was lodging there.

Holmes paced the floor in that familiar fashion, clearly still forming his conclusions based upon the data in his possession.

'Watson, Watson... We have here a most interesting little puzzle. You may have wondered why I could not give you much information after our sojourn to the country. Well, the honest answer is that I could not *find* very much information; not enough, at least, to form a firm hypothesis. I had expected to discover signs of a struggle if the maid really had abducted the parrot – but no – or perhaps the remains of the unfortunate Rodney – but, again, no. I even took the liberty of examining the McMillans' bins in case I may find the parrot's body, but to no avail.'

'So, why have you called me here, Holmes?'

'All will soon be revealed, of that I am sure. First, let me tell you what I have learned up till now.'

'That would be gratifying,' I said with some impatience. Holmes kept walking back and forth and I sensed this commentary was as much for his benefit as for mine, his eyes looking skyward as if searching for definite answers.

'Let us start with the most vital facts.'

'Well, Rodney went missing–'

'No, no. That was my great error. I let the McMillans' priorities lead me in the wrong direction. The most important point is not the parrot, but the silver cutlery that the maid is accused of stealing.

'My first real piece of evidence regarded the driveway. When we arrived at the McMillans' I could see the recent marks of two carriages, aside from our own. The ground was still damp from the weekend rain, you'll remember, and one of these two carriages had the broad, sturdy wheels of the hansom cab, while the others' marks were narrower. When I had my little *reconnoitre* of the grounds, I took the liberty of checking the McMillans' own vehicle and the wheels matched one set of tracks precisely. Yet Carruthers insisted that he had received no visitors while his master and mistress were away, and the staff all walked into the village for their holiday – it's only a mile from the house. So, the question is… who had used the cab?'

'The girl, of course,' I said, surprised at Holmes missing such an obvious point.

'How could she afford it?'

'The cutlery set!' I exclaimed, but Holmes shook his head dismissively.

'Then, how could she have summoned the cab? The house has no telephone.'

'An accomplice perhaps. She had arranged for him to pick her up when Carruthers was at church.'

Holmes looked disappointed again. 'I'm afraid our problem may be more complex than a simple theft. Cast your mind back to her room, Watson. What did you notice?'

'A typical servant girl's quarters, I should imagine. Most of her clothes were missing, of course, and I did not see any bag or case, so she must have packed her belongings and left.'

'You are observing as well as seeing, Watson. Excellent! What else?'

I concentrated on my mental image of the drab room. 'A bed, a coat, a photograph…'

'Precisely, Watson. A photograph of a young family. She had framed it herself and hung it on her wall – her only keepsake of her own deceased parents, I shouldn't wonder – yet she left it when she decided to flee. Why would that be? Why would anyone leave something so personal behind?'

'She must have been in great haste if she was trying to flee with the silverware.'

'Yes, but what would make someone, especially a sentimental young girl of eighteen, run away without taking her most treasured possession? It simply does not compute.'

I conceded that it was indeed odd. It would have taken no effort to put the flimsy picture into a bag, even in a hurry, and it did seem unlikely that she would overlook such an item in that spartan room.

'You observed her overcoat. Why would she leave that?'

'It was a muggy day.'

'It is September, Watson! Would a girl of limited means leave her overcoat if she were planning to escape? Autumn is nearly upon us!' I shook my head, and Holmes pressed his case.

'And then there was the stocking. Now, you are the expert in such matters, Watson.' I flushed and loosened my collar. 'I take it that such an exquisitely-made item is not *de rigueur* among the servant classes.'

'Holmes,' I protested, 'I'm sure I don't know these things…'

'Come, come, Watson. This is no time to be coy. A woman's honour may be at stake, perhaps even her entire future.'

I was shocked by this revelation. 'What on earth do you mean?'

'The stocking, Watson.'

'It certainly looked an expensive variety. No, I would not expect a scullery maid to own such a pair of undergarments.'

'In itself intriguing. And why would Annabel pack one of the pair but not the other?'

'Perhaps she did not have time to check.'

'It was one of the few things left in the drawer. It would have taken but a fraction of a second to pick it up and place it in her bag with her other belongings. No, no… something was most definitely awry in that scenario. So, the question became *why* she would leave in such haste? She would have known that she was alone for a few hours on Sunday morning when Carruthers went to church, and she could have packed a bag in preparation at any time, regardless of others being in the house. No, no… the evidence suggests that she did not *choose* to flee; she was *forced* to. Someone else packed her bag for her.'

'You certainly make a good case,' I conceded, but Holmes was not listening. His words were streaming from his consciousness now, his eyes raised to the heavens, and I knew that he was piecing together all the disparate strands into a coherent whole.

'Something was missing from the narrative, something that we had not been told. That is why I telegraphed Mycroft when we left the estate and asked him about the prime minister's recent movements.'

'The prime–'

'Lord McMillan said that he was with Salisbury at Downing Street on Saturday evening until Sunday morning. Mycroft confirmed that there is indeed a royal scandal brewing, as the lord said, involving one of our young princes and a game of baccarat, I believe.'

'McMillan was telling the truth, then.'

'But the prime minister was attending a private party in Devon all weekend. It was not officially recorded so it is unlikely McMillan would have known of it.'

'He wasn't in Downing Street?'

'Precisely, Watson. I'm glad to see you're taking something in. So, we know that Lord McMillan was lying to his wife, and to us, about his whereabouts overnight on Saturday until lunchtime on Sunday, at around the same time as our maid and the parrot went missing. And we also know that this girl was in possession of an expensive undergarment beyond the means of a country maid. It may be mere coincidence, but it is certainly an intriguing one. Furthermore, it is clear that McMillan was less enthusiastic to see us on Monday than his wife was.'

'I found him a gracious host,' I countered. 'He and his wife were fine company at dinner.'

Holmes ignored my comment. 'I knew that we would not discover anything more of note there. Lord McMillan is a typical politician – shrewd, charming and dangerous. And if we surmise that the maid did not pack her belongings herself... Well, that troubled me, Watson; it troubled me deeply.

'On our return to London, I made inquiries at all the service agencies on Bingham Street, acting in the role of Carruthers.' As he admitted this deceit, he even took on the voice of the sober butler. 'After a number of unsuccessful attempts to "Find a replacement for the last maid you sent to us, young Annabel," I received a positive response from an agent at the Jackson and Jackson agency. I entered into conversation with the delightful Mrs Jackson and, according to her, Annabel Simkins was a bright and exceedingly pretty girl who had recently been orphaned. Her late father was an invalid, an old soldier, and Annabel had nursed him since his return from service. Her mother had died of tuberculosis two years ago, so when she lost her father, she was forced to go out to work. Mrs Jackson was stunned to hear that she may have been involved in any kind of skulduggery.

"'I don't believe it,' she told me very firmly. "I knew Annabel's family personally, that is why I was prepared to vouch for her even without experience. There's no way on God's earth that she would ever do anything to harm anybody, most especially a defenceless animal. As for theft, it's absolutely out of the question." She was quite unmovable on the subject, Watson, and on further investigation, I'm inclined to agree. I spoke to Annabel's old neighbours, and I could not find anyone with a bad word to say about the girl.'

'But where is she now?'

'Her family home was rented and she hasn't returned since her father's death. According to Mrs Jackson she had no other family to speak of, and I could not gain any further information from her old acquaintances.'

'So the trail has gone cold,' I lamented.

'Well, we know that she is from London, and I judged she would likely return to where she knew best. And I had one more card to play... The Ercuis silverware set. She must be a desperate woman and – if she indeed took it – she would need to sell it, or pawn it at the very least, in order to survive. With that in mind, I let it be known among the silver dealers and pawnshops within a five-mile radius of her old residence that Mr Neville Hennessy, that famous timber magnate, was in the market for an original Ercuis '67 set and was prepared to pay any price.' Holmes handed me a visiting card with the name of that fictitious gentlemen, but with Holmes's Baker Street address written beneath it. 'Anybody acting as a broker would receive a handsome fee, but naturally I would wish to speak to the current owner in person, in order to confirm the set's authenticity.'

'This is all very well, Holmes,' I said, 'but what of Rodney? What of Lady McMillan's parrot? Was that not the mystery that you were commissioned to solve?'

'Frankly, Watson, I believe we are too late to save the parrot, but we may just save a young girl from a life in gaol, or perhaps worse. And I am in little doubt that the fate of poor Rodney will be revealed to us in due course.'

I was about to demand an explanation when the front doorbell rang and we heard a young lady's voice introducing herself to the servant boy.

This woman was ushered to our – no, *Holmes's* – rooms where my friend bade her enter. She was singularly beautiful, with long blonde hair and intense, intelligent green eyes. She carried a cloth bag that clattered slightly as she walked. Holmes asked her to sit.

'I prefer to stand, gentlemen.' She fixed her eyes on Holmes, a steady gaze that spoke of a steely resolve. Her bearing was self-contained but I could discern a slight tremor in her voice; she was not used to such dealings, of that I was sure. 'Mr Lentini in Fulham said that you may have a special interest in this silverware. What is your offer, Mr Hennessy?'

'Your freedom, Miss Simkins.'

It took a fraction of a second before the wretched girl realised the consequences of what Holmes had just said. Before she could dash for the door, Holmes was already there, blocking her exit.

'My dear,' he said softly, 'I give you the same assurance I give everyone in your position. If you are honest with me, I guarantee that I shall play a straight bat with you. I am not the official police and my obligation is not to the laws of England. Your safest path is to tell me all, for I already know most of your tale.'

Annabel Simkins fell onto the nearest chair and put her hands on her face. She sighed, then looked up at us with something approaching a smile. 'You're Sherlock Holmes, aren't you?'

It was Holmes's turn to look surprised now. 'Yes. Yes, I am.'

'I thought it strange that a timber baron would choose to live on Baker Street. And there is only one man I know who lives here.' She sensed Holmes's amazement. 'I can read, you know. I've seen your name in the papers.' She turned to me. 'Dr Wilson?'

'Watson,' I corrected.

'I've read some of your accounts. They're very entertaining.'

Holmes grinned at this. In his analytical mind, she had just inflicted the fiercest criticism upon my little dispatches.

Annabel Simkins lifted her head proudly and began her narrative. 'I presume you know my circumstances. My family, my father's death this May. Mrs Jackson at the agency had been an old friend of my mother's and she vowed to help me find a suitable position. She was as good as her word, and I started at the McMillans' in June. It's strange, you know. I've done nothing but cook and clean and tend to my poor dad these last few years, and it never felt a hardship. I wanted to help my family and make them proud. But as soon as I was doing those same tasks for somebody else... I could do it all easily enough, but I just never felt inclined to do it *well*. Carruthers was always scolding me, and Lady McMillan was a relentless old witch. The cooks and other staff, they didn't take to me much; they said I had ideas above my station, too clever for my own good. My only joy was Rodney. One of my duties was to feed and water him, and I would make it last as long as I could each day.

'Lady McMillan... one day she heard me talking to him. Rodney always loved to copy me, anything I said. And her ladyship was actually jealous! Jealous of me taking her Rodney away from her, I think. She would shout at me all the time and blame me for anything she could think of. Her husband, though, he was nice. He always protected me from her and took the time to talk to me. The only one in that house who treated me like... like I was a person. He sometimes gave me little presents, just old clothes or little trinkets he picked up in London. Then... then he started giving me more personal things. He said he wanted me to look nice and feel nice.' She swallowed and looked around, as if unsure whether to continue.

'We saw the kind of things he gave you, Miss Simkins,' Holmes said as he sat down opposite her. His voice was low now. He had a tremendous ability to say just the right words that would encourage the interviewee to continue.

'He started coming to my room sometimes, late at night. "Just for a talk," he said, but he began getting too friendly, you know. I always managed to stop him from doing anything, and I reminded him that Carruthers was just in the next room, but he promised that he would find a way for us to be alone one day. He said he loved me. I thought he was just a silly man saying silly things after too much whisky…

'Still, it came so that I was happy whenever he went down to London. Even with everyone in that house disliking me, it was better than putting up with his nonsense. And last week, when him and her went to town together and they gave the other staff the weekend off… well, it was lovely. I could walk around the house without worrying. All I had to do was avoid old Carruthers. I didn't know then that it was a trap, of course. Lord McMillan had set it all up…

'Me and Rodney were having a grand old time in that jungle room. That's what I called it.' Her smile turned to a scowl. 'Then he came back.'

'Lord McMillan?' I exclaimed.

'Sunday morning. Carruthers had just gone to church, then I heard a carriage arrive, and Lord McMillan staggered in the house – gave me a terrible shock. In his cups, he was, been drinking all night somewhere. I could smell the poppy on him too. He'd taken the morning train all the way back from London. He said he couldn't live without me another day, another night. He was breathing his ghastly breath in my face, pawing at me, trying to make love to me. A horrible thing.

And then I slapped him, really hard, on his ear. He fell to the floor and he went quiet.

'I was scared. I didn't mean to hurt him, but he'd got me in a corner and I just had to get him off me. But now he was lying there, not moving, his eyes closed... I thought he might be dead.

'But then he groaned and started twitching. He opened his eyes and got up – slowly, murder in his eyes. I tried to check he was alright, but he looked at me then with such... hate. He'd got his senses back now. He'd sobered up, and that just made him more frightening. He grabbed my wrist and just kept muttering.

'"I'll kill you, Annabel, I'll kill you, Annabel," he said, again and again, louder and louder, until he was screaming at the top of his lungs. "I'll kill you, Annabel! I'll kill you, Annabel!" He still had my wrist and he was pushing me against the wall, his other hand raised, saying the same words over and over. "I'll kill you, Annabel!" He pushed me to the carpet. I was curled up in the corner, he had me trapped, nowhere to run. I thought he was about to murder me.

'It was silent for a few seconds. I was just waiting for his blow, trying to cover my head. I was sure he was going to...

'Then I heard those words again. "I'll kill you, Annabel. I'll kill you, Annabel." I looked up. It wasn't McMillan. It was Rodney! Squawking them words, just like his master. "I'll kill you, Annabel." Rodney was copying him, mocking him.' Tears formed in the young woman's emerald eyes.

'McMillan hated that. He looked so terrified, like he'd been found out, and Rodney just kept repeating it. Then the lord's expression changed – from fear to hate. He slapped me hard, then he got up and walked over to Rodney. He was sneering now, looking at me the whole time as he opened the cage door.

'"You love Rodney, don't you?" he said.

'And Rodney just kept repeating that same phrase, "I'll kill you, Annabel," in his funny voice. I think… I think that… maybe Rodney knew that he was saving me. Even as McMillan grabbed him by the neck, he kept saying it, taunting him with his guilt. And then McMillan did it…'

'Did what, my dear?'

'He snapped Rodney's neck.'

I gasped at this horrific revelation, at the utter cruelty inflicted upon the defenceless animal and upon this poor girl. She was in a pitiful state now and I gave her my handkerchief then poured her a brandy. This steadied her nerves, and she was indeed a strong character. She was soon able to continue through her tears.

'Lord McMillan left the room, still holding Rodney. I didn't move, I was so shocked. Then he came back with my bag and threw it at me. It had my clothes in it.

'"There's all your things," he screamed at me. "You've got five minutes to get out, or I'll do to you what I did to your little friend." He still had Rodney in his hand. Then he ran off, I didn't know where; the kitchen, perhaps. I was still shaking, I was so frightened…'

'Go on, my dear,' Holmes uttered quietly.

'When I gathered my senses, I knew I had to get out of there. I didn't check my bag, I just picked it up and ran for the front door. I was going to be homeless, in the middle of nowhere. No family, no money, and I was losing my job and my home. That's when I walked past the dining room. I didn't really think, I just went in and grabbed the box of cutlery from the drawer. I knew it was silver, I knew it was worth something. I just shoved the box in my bag, then left by the front entrance. If nothing else, I thought, at least I'm free of that horrible place—

'But he was back. Right behind me. He told me that I wasn't to go into the village, people would ask too many questions. He still had the cab waiting out front; I imagine he'd thought he would have his wicked way then dash straight back to the station and get the return train to London. He smiled at the driver. "I'm just taking this young lady to her mother's," he said, and he pushed me into the back of the cab. Then he squeezed in next to me and told the driver to take us to the station.

'He was still trying to grab me even then, but thankfully it's a short ride into Oxford. The driver kept craning his neck to see us, and his lordship was careful not to cause a scandal, I think.

'At the station, he paid the man with a lot of notes, then he shoved a couple of guinea into my hand. My silence was worth less than the driver's.

"'I never want to see you again," he said, then he ran to catch the express to London. I waited, as you can imagine. I didn't want to see him again either, and I definitely didn't want to be on the same train. But London's all I know, so I used the money to get myself back here later that afternoon, and I've been staying here and there since… a friend's house, a shelter, a church. But I need somewhere to live, and I knew nobody would give me work as a maid again, so I've been trying to get rid of this. It's my only way to get money…' She lifted the bag full of silver cutlery, almost apologetically. 'Oh, Mr Holmes, whatever will happen to me?'

'Miss Simkins, I did not perform this little subterfuge in order to incriminate you,' Holmes said tenderly. 'I performed it in order to help you.'

'Help me?' She was incredulous, as was I. Holmes was a man of honour and decency, but I rarely saw him display kindness so openly, particularly to this poor soul who had, however justifiably, committed theft.

'What do you intend to do, Holmes?' I asked.

'I intend to return the silverware to its rightful owner. In doing so, I hope that I shall make your future a little brighter, my dear.'

On hearing these words, Annabel Simkins' sad features softened and the faintest of smiles crossed her lips.

III. A Shameful Conclusion

The next day, Holmes and I repeated the journey to Oxfordshire and the McMillan estate. My companion was in a melancholy humour and barely spoke until our cab conveyed us in to the grounds of the McMillan house.

'I still cannot fathom what happened to the parrot,' he mused at last. 'I carried out a thorough examination of the grounds on Monday, and I searched the bins too, but there wasn't a scrap to be found.'

'Miss Simkins had no reason to lie,' I said.

'Of course not. But…' Holmes's thought appeared to drift away as we approached the grand Georgian façade of the splendid manor. This time it was Lady McMillan who ran out to meet our carriage, very nearly flattening Carruthers in her rush to receive us.

'Gentlemen,' she exclaimed, 'pray tell what you have learned.'

'My lady,' Holmes replied, 'I'm afraid we do not bring good news.'

It was fortunate that Carruthers was there to catch his mistress as she very nearly fainted. It took all of the butler's strength to support her, but he was able to lead her inside, and Holmes and I strode ahead, my friend carrying a dispatch case.

'We're here to speak to Lord McMillan,' Holmes said forcefully, and walked into the living room without waiting for invitation.

'What is the meaning of this?' barked the man of the house, leaping from the settee upon which he had been perusing the Saturday papers. 'How dare you, gentlemen?!'

'How dare *you*, sir?' Holmes replied, fixing such a stare upon McMillan that the seasoned politician cowered beneath it, sinking back onto his seat. For a few seconds he appeared to be trying to concoct some lie, but Holmes's glare did not waver, and finally the lord bowed his head and his voice came out in a pathetic croak.

'What do you know, Mr Holmes?'

'Enough to give your wife ample grounds for divorce, and you a charge of animal cruelty; not to mention your assault of an innocent young girl.'

'She's a liar!' McMillan hissed petulantly.

'Would you like a court of law to decide that?' Holmes's words extinguished the last embers of fight from his adversary.

'What is it you want, Mr Holmes?'

'Compensation,' my friend answered.

'I did not judge you such a mercenary,' the villain sneered.

'Not for me, McMillan; for Annabel Simkins.' Holmes opened his dispatch case, lifted it upside down and shook the contents onto the bearskin rug.

'The Ercuis!' The voice was Lady McMillan's. She was standing at the threshold to the room alongside Carruthers, staring joyfully at the mess of silverware clattering to the floor. Her husband looked terrified, a frightened child waiting to be scolded by a teacher.

'My dear…' He swallowed, clearly unsure how much she had heard. He breathed a barely perceptible sigh of relief when his wife yelped with happiness.

'Oh, Mr Holmes! However did you find it? Aunt Hattie's wedding present! It's priceless! Priceless!'

'I'm afraid it cost rather a lot to retrieve.' said Holmes. 'I was just discussing terms with your husband.'

'Oh, William will pay. Won't you, dear?'

'Of course, darling,' replied Lord McMillan as he attempted to maintain some vestige of dignity, even as his face turned redder.

'Well… at least we've had *some* good news today,' said Lady McMillan, more forlornly. 'Now, if you'll excuse me, gentlemen, I should lie down.' With that, Carruthers led her out of the room and up the stairs, and Holmes turned back to the lord.

'I believe a hundred pounds is a fair price.'

I was stunned by the amount Holmes suggested, being at least two years' salary for a maid in London, let alone on a rural estate. But I am, of course, a humble physician, and this exalted peer of the realm barely blinked at the number.

'I will write a cheque at once,' he said quietly.

'I require something else' Holmes said, and McMillan raised an eyebrow. 'A reference letter for Miss Simkins.'

'Certainly,' the lord said, with visible relief.

'Oh, and one last thing,' Holmes added.

'What?' A flash of anger betrayed McMillan's dangerous inner strength, and I was concerned that Holmes may push this formidable foe too far.

'Some information, that is all,' assured my friend. 'You commissioned me to find your wife's parrot.'

McMillan was confused by this line of inquiry. 'Yes. I did not have much choice, such was Marcia's insistence.'

'But I have failed,' said Holmes. 'I have not been able to recover Rodney, dead or alive.'

McMillan smirked. 'And you're not likely to do so.'

'I must ask you, sir,' the detective pressed. 'However did you dispose of him? I searched everywhere.'

McMillan looked around conspiratorially, checking that nobody was in earshot. He smiled grimly as he whispered. 'One of my wife's summer hats may have gained... a few more feathers.'

I moved to strike the scoundrel before Holmes placated me with an outstretched arm.

'You fiend!' I seethed, but the politician's ugly grin remained.

'But what of the body?' Holmes asked, more calmly.

Lord McMillan took a deep breath and his chest swelled, as if he sensed that he may gain a small victory at last. I was surprised when he turned his head and addressed not Holmes but myself.

'Dr Watson,' he smirked, 'when you dined with us on Monday evening, I mentioned to you that I liked to cook.' The realisation of what he was telling me chilled me to my very core.

'You monster!' I nearly wretched, but McMillan continued.

'I trust you enjoyed the game soup.'

On the train journey back to the capital, in possession of the cheque and reference letter for Miss Simkins, I was filled with rage and sick to the stomach at the thought of how I had inadvertently assisted in such evil. My anger was the result not only of McMillan's heinous deeds but of my companion's lack of sympathy. In fact, I detected a touch of mirth in Holmes's weak attempts to console me. It was only as we neared Paddington that Holmes finally revealed his *pièce de résistance* and provided me with some solace.

'Come, now, Watson,' he said, noting my indignation. 'McMillan will suffer for what he has done.'

'Really, Holmes?' I'm ashamed to say that I spoke rather too loudly in our shared compartment. I lowered my voice, but my umbrage was still plain for our fellow passengers to see. 'You saw how unconcerned he was about a hundred pounds. To men like him, such paltry figures are but a minor irritation.'

'I went to the Diogenes Club yesterday evening after we met the delightful Miss Simkins.'

'Oh?' I grunted. I was still bitter at my role in the dreadful case.

'I told Mycroft about his lordship's crimes.'

I rallied a little at this development. 'What did he say?'

'He was shocked, of course. Mycroft has known McMillan for many years. However, for all my brother's political nous, he is a man of honour. He went to Salisbury immediately to discuss a suitable course of action.'

'McMillan will be relieved of his position?' I asked with some enthusiasm, and Holmes put his finger to his lips, urging me to be quiet.

'It would not do for one of the government's most prominent statesmen to be dismissed so suddenly. Questions would be asked, and Salisbury is keen to avoid being pulled into a scandal.'

I was apoplectic now. 'The coward! The swine!'

'Now, now, my dear fellow,' said Holmes with a gentle pat of my hand. 'McMillan's fate is to be much worse than dismissal. Mycroft tells me that the prime minister will offer McMillan a new post abroad instead, and that due to budgetary concerns, his wife should remain in England.'

'Well, that's something,' I conceded. 'But to his kind, no doubt it will just be an opportunity to carouse even more freely with the local population.'

'Not where he is going,' said Holmes and the edge of his mouth curled up into a wicked smile. 'He is to be the new governor—'

'Governor?!' I snorted at the sheer injustice of it all. This perpetrator of unforgivable acts, who had the ear of the prime minister himself, was now to gain a position of even greater power in the Empire.

'He will be governor,' Holmes continued, 'of South Georgia, just off Antarctica. Population… Three.'

The Montmartre Murders

Covering Note to *The Montmartre Murders*

As the country lurches from perhaps its blackest winter into this rather grey and dreary spring of nineteen-seventeen, one could be forgiven for thinking the dark clouds I observe now from the study window are wisps of smoke from our army's present battles on the continent. It is strange how every Englishman has recently become well versed in the geography of northern Europe, with the place names of the Somme, Flanders, Ypres, and Mametz etched into our national consciousness – places that will forever be associated with incalculable loss and sacrifice.

Just yesterday, I received an unexpected but very welcome visit from my dear friend, Mr Sherlock Holmes. It had been some time since we had enjoyed one another's acquaintance, so there was much on which to catch up, and yet, very soon, our conversation turned to events in France, with the battle of Arras currently the focus of national attention.

Holmes reminded me of his own time in France, during his three-year hiatus when he disappeared from public view, presumed perished at Reichenbach, though actually travelling the world to avoid any vengeful acolytes of his old foe, Moriarty. It has been a quarter of a century since but, strangely, we have rarely talked about that most curious period in his life, when he travelled to places as far flung as the Himalayas. There has developed a tacit agreement between us not to dwell on that period when I felt most bereft at the loss of my companion, only to then experience the simultaneous relief and betrayal of his sudden reappearance.

I was keen to hear more of his experiences in France. Much to Holmes's annoyance, I insisted on our moving to the same study in which I am sat now, scrambling for pen and paper in order to chronicle this previously untold story. I knew he had conducted some scientific research in the south of the country but knew little of his short sojourn in Paris. I wrote feverishly as he relayed the details of his adventures in the French capital.

On completion of his tale, though, I wished I had never pressed him to tell it, for the details within caused my skin to crawl, and for me to question the very morality of Man… and even the very morality of Sherlock Holmes.

Presently, as I look out from my window and onto my modest garden, the lawn a most verdant green and the bulbs and roses straining into life against the greyness of a reluctant spring, I can finally dare imagine a world unstained by war. Recent news that our friends in America have joined the fight alongside our allies from Canada and the Antipodes, has filled the country with fresh hope. Perhaps I can also dare imagine a world unsullied by the dark actions narrated by Holmes in his telling of the Montmartre murders.

I write this following story from the point-of-view of Sherlock Holmes. Unlike most of our other adventures, I was thankfully not present and so I act merely as scribe, dictated this most sordid tale, and bear no responsibility for the events that occurred within.

John H. Watson, M.D.
22nd April 1917

I. A Holiday in Paris

Some of the Parisians I met despised the Eiffel Tower. It was four years since it was opened and visitors still came daily in their thousands to scale its three-hundred-foot frame. Admirers marvelled at its audacious design, its multitudinous wrought iron struts giving it the air of a magnificent matchstick creation, almost daring any strong wind to blow it down. And yet its local critics remained convinced that its modernity had forever scarred the city's skyline.

While I strongly disagreed with their assertion that the tower was nothing more than a faddish monstrosity, I rather admired the obdurate standpoint of some of the elderly regulars in the café I frequented most days in that autumn of 1893.

I had found modest but comfortable lodgings on Rue Ordener, situated in the city's eighteenth *arrondisement*, to the north of the great hill of Montmartre. It was a bustling area of greengrocer shops and boulangeries catering handsomely for its lower-middle-class residents. The goods on offer were inexpensive and unpretentiously presented, and yet the sweetness of the golden apples and the doughy aroma of the freshly-baked bread were unlike anything one would find in London, even for a handsome fee.

As you know, Watson, I had concealed my true identity with an almost fierce paranoia ever since fleeing the scene of my supposed death at Reichenbach. I have told you previously that I had adopted the persona of a Norwegian adventurer while travelling through Tibet but felt that a Scandinavian explorer would attract too much attention if he were to turn up in the backstreets of Paris! Instead, I took on the visage of a doctor from Bordeaux, taking a brief sabbatical from his duties to enjoy the culture of his nation's great capital. I pride myself on my unaccented French, though it has been mentioned on more than one occasion in the past that my intonation is that of a native speaker from the south-west, so playing a *Girondin* was a logical decision.

I very quickly became accepted into the local community, and, with nothing to do during daytime hours, I was adopted by the retired locals who chatted, griped and argued over cups of excellent coffee served in Monsieur Ferri's café not far from my rooms. Embarrassingly, the older men were all too happy to share with me their every ache or malady when they took me to be a doctor. Thankfully, thanks to our many years together, Watson, I was able to offer convincing remedies for their minor ailments. In fact, there was something liberating about living incognito, and I am ashamed to say I would occasionally think of you as my muse, considering what my old companion from Baker Street would do in certain situations. It was thanks to this deliberate shift in character that I allowed myself to enjoy the cultural life of *la Ville Lumière* a little more than I ordinarily would. There was little for me to do by way of work and so I endeavoured to live the life of a normal educated gentleman holidaying in one of the world's great cities.

Rue Ordener is on the side of the Montmartre hill that is furthest away from the grand new boulevards of the metropolis's heart. From the middle of Paris, the city's avenues appear to slope upwards towards Montmartre on the horizon, the sun gleaming on the white travertine stone that made up the then half-finished basilica of the Sacré-Coeur. It is the perfect place for a church, as close to the heavens as nature will allow. The other side of Montmartre where I lived, however, seemed to be perpetually in shade, rather fitting for a man in hiding like me.

Every day, I would climb the hill's stone steps in order to gain a most splendid view of Paris. I would be joined by two of the most recalcitrant members of my café gang, a Monsieur Renard and a Monsieur Maurier. With the autumn leaves freshly fallen, our panoramic view of the city from the top of Montmartre was unfettered by foliage, and so all of Paris lay out in front of us like a lightly ruffled blanket. Of course, my companions' indignant attention was focused solely on the metallic edifice to the south-west. The Eiffel Tower rose like a lighthouse protecting the city from the complacency of the past.

You know I am not a man naturally predisposed towards the aesthetic, and yet I was daily spellbound by both the tower's beauty and by the engineering achievement it represented.

It was a triumph of the contemporary, and yet – where we stood at the summit of the hill – a Catholic church was fast being built, directly behind us, much preferred by the conservative Renard and Maurier to Eiffel's creation, but a shameless throwback to another era.

'At least the Sacré-Coeur will serve a purpose,' grumbled Renard, before turning back to the tower in the distance. 'Not like that-… that-… tribute to man's vanity over there.'

One morning, my friends and I were joined in the café by a fellow I had not previously met. When he entered, he had nodded his familiar *bonjour*s to the other men and to Monsieur Ferri, so I took him to be local. He was a studious, slightly nervous gentleman wearing round-rimmed spectacles, glued together at the bridge, that pinched against his nose. He was only in his forties and yet he walked with a pronounced limp and leaned on a crutch. He joined us at our nest of chairs in the corner of the room. I presented myself under my alias, while he was introduced to me as Maximilian Cauvain.

'Or *Professor* Cauvain, should I say?' I asked as I shook his hand.

He was momentarily disarmed by my knowledge of his title.

'Excuse our nosy friend,' laughed Renard. 'It is something of a hobby of his, to guess who you are, what you do, and what you had for breakfast – all by just looking you up and down.'

'He should be on the stage on La Pigalle with this circus trick!' added Maurier.

'It's no trick, gentlemen,' I stated. 'Merely logic. Seeing what others choose not to see.'

'I'm fascinated,' Cauvain smiled warmly. 'So how do you know I'm a professor?'

'You are of working age and yet it is a Monday. I have read that the universities are now to close one day a week – a sanction just recently imposed by the government following the student protests some weeks ago.'

Renard and Maurier collectively tutted at mention of the students' dissent. 'Damned anarchists...' Maurier muttered.

I continued: 'The lenses in your spectacles, I notice, are to counter long-sightedness. Few perceive this as a malady – not unless your living comes from reading books, so I'm going to wager you are a man of letters. A professor of literature, perhaps?'

'*Mon dieu*,' said Cauvain, shaking his head ruefully. I sensed the other men's delight in this side-show.

'Indeed, the very fact you have continued to fix the same pair of reading glasses indicates how important they are to you and your livelihood.'

Cauvain clapped me. 'Bravo!'

'And you are a veteran of the Franco-Prussian War, are you not?'

I sensed the professor's mood change. He was serious for a moment. Not angry, but sad.

'Cauvain here is a good man,' Maurier interrupted. 'A true hero.'

Feeling Cauvain's reluctance to discuss his past, I decided not to elaborate on the thinking behind my observation. However, he himself asked me how I had deduced his history.

'My apologies, my friend, if I have offended you,' I said. 'The crutch you use is basic army issue. Ash wood. However, beech is used more often now – or metal, even. So I took it that you were injured in a skirmish of some years past. Your age led me to conclude it was in combat with the Prussians twenty years ago. An educated assumption.'

Cauvain laughed, his mood suddenly lifted. 'You are extraordinary, sir. But can you tell me what I had for breakfast, like Renard says you can?'

'The croissants and coffee Monsieur Ferri is bringing to our table now, I should imagine.' The room guffawed, though I confess I had not meant it as a joke.

Later that morning, Cauvain asked if he could join our little gang for our daily walk up the steps of Montmartre. I was happy for his company.

I noticed the pain etched across his brow as we slowly made our way up the steep incline. It was clear his war injuries had been significant. It was the middle of October and yet the sun was warm. The effort required for him to make the ascent was evident.

When we reached the top, we settled for an outside table at a narrow café in Montmartre's bustling town square, Place du Tertre. Renard and Maurier continued to argue about the growing volume of artists setting up easels on the pavements while Cauvain caught his breath.

The professor perused a copy of *Le Figaro* newspaper, left on our table by a previous customer. There was little of note on the front page, but his attention was caught by a shorter story on the inside pages, reporting the sudden disappearance of half a dozen dogs in and around Montmartre. Police, the report said, suspected the kidnappings to be the work of a dog-fighting ring, probably in Belleville.

'A curious case, don't you agree?' Cauvain muttered. 'My landlady had a dog that went missing just last week.'

'You think it's being used as a fighting animal?' I asked.

'I doubt it, my friend. It is a tiny poodle – it could barely kill a mouse!'

'Maybe it's being used as bait,' ventured Maurier.

'Perhaps. There was something strange about its disappearance though,' said the professor. 'It was taken from my landlady's apartment upstairs from mine – and yet they left her expensive ornaments and even her jewellery... I would have presumed that burglars wanting a dog for fighting might also have taken some valuables at the same time. But it was only the dog that was gone... and there was one more thing...'

We leaned in closer. Cauvain took a breath. 'She owned a photograph – of her late husband, killed in 1871... a member of the National Guard. There was a red mark daubed across his face in the picture.'

'National Guard?!' scoffed Renard. 'You mean her husband was a socialist conspirator?'

I recalled that members of the National Guard were instrumental in the Communard uprising, when Paris briefly slipped under socialist rule.

'I don't like to see the deceased dishonoured,' Maurier continued, 'but the only good socialist, in my view, is a dead one.'

I considered what motive might lead a villain to steal a dog from an elderly widow, and what message he was sending with the defaced photograph.

'Do you know the identity of any of the other victims of these dog thefts?' I asked. 'Are they all nearby?'

'I know Madame Hulot lost hers,' remembered Renard. 'She's on Rue Marcadet.'

'And Madame Poesy,' added Maurier. 'She's the flower-seller on Rue Gabrielle, just round the corner from here. Her Pyrenean mountain dog would be good in a fight! He soon scared off anyone thieving her tulips!'

'And are either of them married?' I enquired.

'No, both of them widows of some years,' said Maurier with a mischievous smile. 'Much to the relief of old Renard here in the case of Madame Poesy! And even better news, now, eh, Renard – because he was terrified of that dog!'

'You speak rubbish, Maurier,' Renard countered forcefully, though his blushes betrayed him.

I picked up the lunch menu. 'Well, perhaps, Monsieur Renard, you could introduce me to Madame Poesy once we've dined. I should like to ask her some questions.'

'Perhaps I could accompany you, Doctor,' said Cauvain. It took me a moment to remember that he was addressing me using my *nom de guerre*.

'Of course, Professor Cauvain,' I replied. There was something about his academic curiosity that I liked and I felt he possessed the sensitivity required for such an exchange with a widow who had lost a much-loved pet. He reminded me a little of you, Watson, in his sensibility.

As we dined on a fine rabbit *cassoulet*, and returned to arguing over architecture and the new wave of artists in Montmartre, I confess to enjoying the bonhomie of our peculiar group. I felt happy – though perhaps that was as much owed to the fact that, after so long reflecting and researching while in hiding, it was finally time to turn my energies to solving what I thought would be nothing more than a curious little case. I have rarely been so wrong.

II. The Dogs of Sacré-Coeur

Madame Poesy's flower shop was a blazing splash of colour among the faded grey buildings on Rue Gabrielle. It was a charming wood-fronted store situated at the bottom of some stone steps that led from Place du Tertre. Its doors and windows were thrown wide open to the world, row upon row of flowers of all colours seeming to roll out onto the avenue.

Maximilian Cauvain took a long sniff of a pink-white posy, just as a woman sashayed outside. It struck me what a fitting name the proprietor bore.

'Madame Poesy. *Enchantez.*' Renard keenly offered his hand.

Madame Poesy shook his hand gently, then turned to face all four of us. She eyed us with suspicion. 'Good afternoon, gentlemen. How may I help you?'

She was a handsome woman, perhaps just shy of her fiftieth year, dressed neatly in the modern fashion – long skirts and tailored jacket – and her hair still a youthful light-brown. She looked solemn, as if lost in thought.

I introduced myself, along with Cauvain. My companion began the questioning: 'We must apologise, Madame, for this intrusion, but we wondered if we could ask you some questions about your missing dog?'

The colour flushed even further from her face as she considered our intentions.

'I'm sorry, Madame Poesy, it was not my idea,' grovelled Renard.

Madame Poesy retained a stoic, almost noble countenance, but something clearly troubled her. 'I can only tell you what I told the police. The dog stolen – he was a strong animal, it would have taken two or three men, at least.'

Renard nodded in agreement.

'Which is why it is strange that they should go to so much bother-…' she paused, incredulous. 'Why would they go through my husband's things first, before taking the dog. My late husband…'

'Your late husband's things?' asked Cauvain. 'You mean they took something else?'

'No, no,' she replied. 'Everything was left just where it was, but his robes – his professor's robes …they were slashed. Still hanging in the armoire – but slashed many, many times.'

Professor Cauvain and I exchanged a glance.

'A professor? What did he teach?' asked Cauvain.

'Philosophy, monsieur,' she replied. 'In the Faculty of Letters at the Sorbonne.'

'Auguste Poesy?!' gasped Cauvain. 'I met him once – he was a fine man, Madame.'

'I agree with you,' she replied, 'but he also had enemies. His writings were distinctly *untraditional*, especially about the Church.'

'He was adamant that religion and democracy should be separated,' said Cauvain.

Renard stifled his reaction, concentrating only on comforting the woman. He took her hand. 'So, they leave everything here, only to steal the dog?'

Madame Poesy pulled her hand away. 'Not *just* to steal the dog… I was visited just an hour ago by two *gendarmes*. They came to tell me that the dog has been found…'

'What a relief, Madame!' exclaimed Maurier, but her silent pause quelled any initial enthusiasm.

'The animal was found dead, gentlemen.' She took a moment to compose herself. 'Killed in the most macabre way, a way I find hard to explain…'

Her voice cut off suddenly. Cauvain found a short stool among the flower boxes and rested it behind Madame Poesy for her to sit.

'I'm sorry, gentlemen…' She formed her words carefully, scarcely believing what she was about to utter. 'It seems my dog was *crucified.*'

The last word hung in the air, none of us fully comprehending it. The thought of a crucified beast was almost preposterous, laughable even.

'I'm sorry, Madame. I'm not sure I fully understand…' Cauvain assumed he had misheard.

'He was found splayed open like-… like a chicken to be roasted, then nailed onto a cross…'

My three friends uttered their revulsion and condolences while my brain processed the information. As you will know, Watson – and, indeed, you have scolded me for on more than one occasion – my mind bypassed the lady's emotional turmoil and went straight to the mystery at hand.

'Where was the dead animal found, Madame?' I asked abruptly.

'Why, not two hundred yards from here…' she said quietly, then looked up towards the top of Montmartre. She had to almost dare herself to look in that direction, then pointed at the white stone and scaffolding that made up the foundations of the half-completed Sacré-Coeur cathedral. 'At the church, messieurs. My dog was crucified at the church, along with five other canines…'

Renard and Maurier stayed with Madame Poesy while Cauvain and I rushed to the building site just a short distance above. I forgot my partner's injury for a moment as I skipped up the dozen or so stone steps. Impatiently, I waited for the professor to limp up.

We approached the church's foundations and immediately saw three policemen busying around. It's funny that, despite the differences in language and uniform, the mannerisms and behaviour of the jobbing policeman are alike the world over. There was even a rather pug-nosed gentleman in plain clothes dishing out the orders, who reminded me of our old friend Inspector Lestrade. For a moment, I mused if Lestrade's French name might lead us to assume he had a cousin on the Parisian force!

We introduced ourselves to him. His name was Inspector Diomede and he was quick to impose his authority upon us and the situation. 'This is a crime scene and no place for tourists,' he blustered angrily.

I told him I was a doctor willing to assist in any initial enquiries, while Cauvain mentioned his acquaintance to Madame Camus, his landlady, to convince Diomede of our credentials.

We were led beneath the impressive three-arched portico of Sacré-Coeur and into the main building. Wooden scaffolds dominated the inside of the vast church, the basilica many years from completion at that time. It was an enormous, cavernous space, still free of the gaudy extravagances one associates with Catholic cathedrals and which, no doubt, adorn it to-day as I recite this unpleasant tale.

Some more police officers stood to attention as the surly inspector guided us to the back of the hall. As the officers parted, a horrible view was revealed to us. It was a shocking and sinister sight.

Six dogs nailed onto six-foot crucifixes, their limbs broken backwards to angle their bodies onto the crosses. In some cases, their stomachs had split open under the pressure of being stretched, innards seeping from their bellies.

Cauvain grabbed his handkerchief and held it to his mouth to block out the stench. The flies had discovered the cadavers and were already feasting on their flesh. He took a breath before stepping forward to examine them more closely. He immediately stepped towards the body of a poodle, presumably that of his landlady.

'*Sacré bleu...*' he said, almost imperceptibly before retreating from the church.

I stayed and pressed Inspector Diomede for more details. 'Whoever did this,' he said, 'is a most cowardly felon. Every one of the owners is a woman, all widows living alone save for their pets.'

'Interesting...' I muttered involuntarily, as I examined one of the bodies.

'Pardon, Doctor?' Diomede enquired.

'I was wondering, Inspector, if I may take the names of the dog owners,' I said, before concluding with a lie: 'As a doctor well trained in the treatment of shock, I may be able to offer these poor widows some comfort.'

It was important for me to conceal my investigative motives, for fear of any questions that may lead to my being identified as Sherlock Holmes. Diomede thought for a moment, before begrudgingly ordering a constable to provide me with names and addresses of the women.

Two thickset constables stepped forward to remove the dogs from their crosses. A large black-eyed Alsatian was pulled clumsily from its crucifix, an eight-inch nail falling to the floor.

'We have enough evidence from the scene, Doctor,' said Diomede, 'so we must take these things away before Bishop Montague returns. He demands this blasphemous scene is removed as quickly as is possible.'

I waited for the inspector to turn away, then bent over to pick up the fallen nail. I wiped the blood with my handkerchief before wrapping the nail and placing it in my coat pocket.

I found Cauvain outside. He was a little sheepish following his episode of squeamishness. 'Forgive me, Doctor,' he said, 'but such scenes often remind me of what I saw twenty years ago.'

I looked around, sure no-one was in earshot. 'You were part of the Commune, were you not, Cauvain? The Communard uprising – it's where you received your injury...?'

Cauvain's eyes widened with fear. He desperately did not want such a statement broadcast in public. He hurried me away, then turned into a tiny alcove where he was confident we were alone. 'Never mention that, Doctor!' he said in a whispered bark. 'Never! Do you hear me?! How did you know?'

'It is your crutch. A man with a full military pension would have had his stick replaced for him – yet yours is battered and repaired many times over. It's clear you have been denied the financial support received by other veterans of war.'

Cauvain considered his options. For a moment, I thought he might run.

'Cauvain, my friend. You misunderstand me...' I tried to persuade him. 'I bear no ill will.'

'But *they* will – Renard and Maurier if they knew, anyone in that church... even the police.'

'And Madame Camus – your landlady... her husband was part of the Commune too, I presume?'

Cauvain's anger began to calm, satisfied I was no enemy. He nodded. 'Francois Camus-... he was my superior in the National Guard. He asked for his wife to offer me lodgings should I ever need them. The life of a college professor has not been easy in Paris these past two decades and so I was in desperate need of a room. The government is suspicious of academia – it fears another revolution – and so it pays poorly in order that few of us stay.'

My mind was cast back to the student protests in the city just two months previous. They were quashed quickly, though it was a shot to the bows for the establishment. The rise of the Communards was still fresh in the city's mind and so any hint of radicalism was stamped out swiftly.

Cauvain quietly relayed his story. He had joined the National Guard as a young man. He had, as I had surmised in the café that morning, fought in the Franco-Prussian War. As you will recall, Watson, that conflict ended with Paris eventually falling to the Germans. Paris had been an unhappy city for some time, with many still believing the Church held too much power over matters of state. Once the Prussians left, the city was a political tinderbox – and with the French government having fled Paris, the working classes and left-wing elite sensed the moment to seize power, and to finally make changes to the lives of ordinary people. The National Guard – with Cauvain amongst them – took the side of the socialist revolt, going into battle against the establishment's army and, for a brief time, coming out on top.

A new Commune was created, one in which the Catholic Church was separated from matters of politics and public welfare – something that pleased the ordinary working people, though predictably horrified the conservative factions of religion and the gentry.

The Communard government was short-lived, however, when the army gathered its forces and outnumbered the National Guard several times over. The so-called Bloody Week of May 1871 saw many hundreds of Communard supporters killed. In return, the Communards executed the Archbishop of Paris.

One of the bloodiest battles of that week, Cauvain told me, was on the very spot where we stood – Montmartre defended by National Guardsmen and civilians, until they were overrun by the army and defeated, the day ending with three hundred prisoners publicly executed.

'It was here that I raised my hands in surrender,' Cauvain told me, looking out from where we stood across the plateau at the peak of Montmartre. 'I had been shot in the leg – the injury that curses me to this day, so I was unable to run. But I was lucky, spared execution only because of a regular soldier who took my gun but shepherded me away before his less forgiving comrades arrived... It is peculiar how two armies are hated enemies, yet two men face-to-face become ordinary humans. I owe him my life. I hid in the cellar of a tavern for three days before it was finally safe to emerge.'

As you know, Watson, I am not a political person, believing that a methodical mind should be above matters of opinion and philosophy, for there should be only fact. I admit, though, to feeling some sympathy for Cauvain and his comrades in their struggle of two decades earlier. I am certain, though, that were I to converse with a survivor of the opposite ideology in that fight, then they too could report similar tales of mistreatment by their enemy, equally convinced of their righteous cause.

My mind was less alert to the politics, as it was piqued by the connection of that ill-fated revolution with the day's slaying of six dogs.

I told Cauvain of my plans to interview the other widows. He approved of my intentions, seemingly regaining some of his lustre. He asked if he could join me.

We moved from the nook in the hill with some purpose, Cauvain studying the list of addresses to decide which one we should visit first. He swiftly noticed one of them was close by and so we made haste.

Our stride was broken almost immediately, though, by the sound of a scream! It was a scream that caused all the pedestrians on Montmartre to freeze in their tracks. A scream that told us something deeply disturbing had just occurred…

III. Death Imitating Art

The man's body was twisted in the most grotesque fashion. His left hand was nailed into the giant cross behind his right ear, and his opposite hand vice versa. He was like a carelessly discarded ragdoll, yet rather than being scattered on the floor, a dozen long nails held his corpse upright on the crucifix. The cross had been hastily made, a crude construction made of two planks from the builders' site behind Sacré-Coeur.

Bizarrely, a freshly-painted artist's canvas leaned against its base. It had been placed there very deliberately.

'May the lord have mercy on his soul!' wailed a beggar woman.

Cauvain and I approached. We were on a narrow bending alleyway that snaked around the church and back towards the busy streets and square. Few people would naturally pass this way, but a small crowd was gathering, their gasps and cries filling the air. Inspector Diomede and the police had yet to arrive, but they would be here from the basilica at any moment.

The victim was a young man dressed in artist's smock splashed with spots of paint. I vaguely recognised his face and so assumed he must be one of the many artists I would have seen plying his trade at the top of the hill. Montmartre had become a haven for these individuals as well as for the modern artistic movements that were bubbling up within the Parisian cultural scene.

I attempted to pull one of the nails from the wood — I proposed to check if its length and metal matched those used on the dogs. Each nail, though, was stuck fast in the structure.

Cauvain leant down — at first, I thought, to pray, until I realised he was studying the painting at the foot of the cross. 'Doctor...' he said, lifting up the picture.

The painting was squarely in the modern style, all clean edges and structural figures... but it depicted a cartoonish Christ-like figure, his limbs twisted around his head, his body nailed to a crucifix. The young man above had been twisted into the exact same pose.

'*Oui*...' Cauvain looked up at the victim's smooth face, no older than twenty. 'I thought so. Claude Giannini... I have seen him working here. He painted this picture. He was a promising artist, very promising, but bold — certainly not to everyone's taste.'

'Any connections with the Communards?' I asked, desperately trying to find a link between the crimes.

'None,' said Cauvain. 'His parents are Italian. They moved here since seventy-one. They run a restaurant — a respectable family but not political.'

'So, we can assume he was murdered purely for his art.'

Cauvain and I waited for Diomede. He greeted my presence with a resigned sigh. Convinced of my medical credentials, the inspector allowed me to examine the body once the area had been cordoned off. The victim's bones had been bent and broken, just like the canines in the church. More care had clearly been taken than with the animals, for where the artist's skin had ripped open, the murderer had stitched it skilfully back together. This was less to preserve young Giannini's integrity in death as it was to hold the corpse in its contorted position and to better replicate the victim's macabre cartoon.

It was clear that the man's throat had been cut, a grim, red line stretching across his neck. There were strange nicks in the thin line of blood, though, about two inches apart; small blotchy dots.

I asked Diomede for the use of any tool – a knife or a crowbar – to prise a nail from the wood. 'It may help if I were able to inspect the limb were it restored to its normal position, Inspector.'

The policeman eyed me a moment, then reached into his capacious coat pocket, pulling out a handsome flick-knife with a smooth ivory handle. 'Here, use this,' he snorted. It was certainly a step up from the functional tools employed by the constabulary in London, with an ornate design scored into the ivory, allowing for a better grip.

I jimmied out a nail, guiding it through the wood of the cross and the bone and sinew in Giannini's limp ankle, until it fell to the floor. Again, when the inspector was turned, I placed the nail in the same handkerchief as the other one that had held up one of the dogs.

After some time examining the scene, it was clear there was no witness to the crime, the body and cross only discovered when an unsuspecting workman had removed part of the fencing around the building site. The body was fresh, however, so the murder could only have happened in the previous few hours.

'Bishop Montague insisted we begin work on the west wing this very day,' stammered the builder. 'We are already behind and so it had to begin to-day…'

Satisfied I had gleaned what I could from the crime scene, Cauvain and I continued our investigation by visiting the remaining widows who had lost their dogs.

We managed to speak to two of the women, both visibly shocked by their experiences. The first had been married to the leader of a small Communist reading group, while the second was another National Guard widow. The mystery was beginning to add up, with all the women's dead husbands connected to movements that could be seen as a threat to the Church's power in French society.

When it came to the fifth widow – a Madame Blanchard – Cauvain baulked when he read her name on the list.

'You know her?' I asked.

'Er, indirectly. Most of the men in the eighteenth *arrondisement* know her…' he replied sheepishly.

Madame Blanchard managed her own successful business on the northern slope of the hill. On first view, it appeared to be a quiet salon. A handful of afternoon drinkers were there when we arrived, but the many tables still sticky with drink from the previous night, and the numerous waitresses cleaning them, indicated a place that would be abuzz with revellers come the evening.

'Maximilian!' cried an elderly woman as she emerged from a back room. My friend's face flooded a bright puce. 'It's been a long time! ...And you've brought me a friend!'

The face powder caked over her wrinkles, the plunging neckline revealing a sagging décolletage, the jet-black wig shifting slightly on her head... It was clear, Watson, that Madame Blanchard was a *madame* in every sense of the term.

She poured us a drink and invited us to sit at the only clean table. As we discussed her slaughtered pet, a trickle of top-hatted gentleman would appear from an internal door before scuttling for the street. Then, in turn, the drinkers in the bar would disappear in their place. All but one of them – a man in a long grey topcoat, too thick to be comfortable in the mild autumn weather, especially indoors, remained. He was a broad, handsome man with flecks of grey in his dark hair, and a golden tan. He stared sullenly into nowhere.

'I have no connections with any anarchists, gentlemen. Well, nothing political, anyway,' Madame Blanchard's eyes twinkled. 'My husband neither – rest his soul. He didn't die for any cause – he was enjoying my company when he passed. Not the first man to go that way, I tell you... But, no, I'm not a red, though I've got nothing against them. Nothing against anyone. I will gladly accept the franc of any socialist, conservative, Christian, Moor or Jew, so long as they pay the right price for my girls.'

'Then why did they kill your animal?' Cauvain mused. 'There must be a pattern...'

Her relaxed, coquettish demeanour vanished for a moment and I detected a flicker in her eyes – towards the bar and the swarthy man in the grey coat. It was if she were seeking his approval.

'Mistaken identity,' she pondered. 'Or probably just street urchins playing a cruel prank…'

'You have no known enemies, Madame?' I asked.

'Perhaps one or two cuckolded wives, but no-one who would do such a thing to my dog.'

It was soon evident there was little else we would discover from further examination. She insisted we did not pay for our drinks, so I offered to at least take the glasses back to the counter. I lay them down and turned for the door, gently nudging against the grey-coated fellow. '*Excusez-moi, monsieur!*' I apologised as his coat gaped open at the neck.

He waved me away grumpily before Cauvain and I exited onto the street.

'As I thought, Cauvain…' We hurried away from the salon. 'The gentleman at the counter with the tan – he was wearing a dog-collar under that coat.'

'A priest?!' exclaimed Cauvain. 'In there?!'

'They are as corruptible as any man,' I smiled, 'though I don't believe he was there for his own leisure. I think he was making sure she didn't reveal too much.'

'Do you think she might have Communard connections, Doctor?'

'No. I have long studied the gestures that give a person away when they are lying. Madame Blanchard's eyes were focused and her breathing easy when she answered those questions about her political leanings, or lack of them… It was only when we directly asked who may have done such a thing to her dog, that she displayed signs of stress common in one who is not telling the truth, or who is concealing something.'

The last widow was an Arab woman from Morocco. She went by the name of Salima Perez. She was reluctant to let us cross the threshold into her home, a small room wedged between a butcher's shop and a tobacco store. She was younger than the other women we had met, still in her thirties, and she had three small children living with her who would occasionally steal a glance at Cauvain and me on the doorstep.

'I don't know why they would do such a thing to our dog,' she said softly, not wanting to alert her children to any distress. 'My children – they are devastated. They have not long lost their father, and now this-… My husband passed away last year – but he was not an enemy of France.'

Madame Perez explained that her husband was a lieutenant in the Spanish army, a decade her senior, and they had met while he was on duty in Morocco. They fell in love and wished to marry, but their union was rejected by her parents in northern Africa and by his family back in Seville. Effectively exiled, Lieutenant Perez and his new wife fled to Paris to begin a new life together. So committed was her husband to his wife that he had converted to the Islamic faith. His death the previous winter had been from influenza.

Although we slowly began to gain her trust, Salima Perez remained cautious of our presence. The tension, though, was broken somewhat when a cherubic face appeared from around her back.

'*Maman?*' Salima Perez's daughter asked. 'Is it the pope again?'

Salima ushered her child inside, shaking her head. She turned back to us: 'I am sorry, but you are not the first men to visit us today.'

'You were visited by a priest also?' I pushed. 'A man in his middle years, with a dark complexion?'

Salima checked the street and thought for a moment. Quickly, she nodded. 'Please, you must go now. It is not me I worry for, but I must protect my children.'

'Very well, Madame Perez,' said Cauvain warmly. 'We understand. *Salam.*'

By now, the sun was dipping behind the brow of Montmartre, long shadows disappearing into darkness. As we turned from the Perez home, I saw a broad-shouldered figure in long grey coat flit swiftly down a side street. The priest from Madame Blanchard's establishment had followed us.

Rather than pursuing the elusive clergyman, I led Cauvain in the opposite direction. We needed as much distance between us and him as possible. I had a plan and we needed to implement it fast.

It was night-time now and we had taken some time to digest our thoughts and for me to briefly return to my rooms to collect my revolver. I had advised Cauvain to do the same.

We re-met outside Monsieur Ferri's café, now closed for the day. 'The connection between all the victims – the widows, young Giannini – is clear,' I explained. 'They are all the perceived enemies of the Church. Socialists, an artist and satirist, the madame of a brothel representing the decline of the city's moral fibre… and finally a woman of the Muslim faith.'

'And that priest getting to Madame Blanchard and Salima Perez confirms this,' Cauvain added.

I pulled out the two identical long nails I had sequestered in the handkerchief in my pocket earlier, one from the dogs and the other used on Giannini. I had cleaned them in my apartment. 'Look at these, Cauvain… I believe these will lead us closer to our murderer.'

He examined them, then looked at me quizzically. I explained: 'Regular iron nails – typically used for any kind of carpentry… But, now, look at the heads of the nails…'

Cauvain looked again and ran his thumb against them. 'They're gold!'

'Gold-plated, to be precise,' I corrected him. 'Used typically for the coffins of the bourgeoisie. The metal used for the length of the nail is concealed so the material is of no importance, yet the heads of the nails will be in full view on the casket, and so gold is used.'

'So, what are you saying?' asked Cauvain.

'When I examined Giannini, I noticed the delicate slices to his body, and the finesse of the stitching – clearly carried out with a scalpel and steady hand. Then there was the way the bones were manipulated to create that grotesque form... Achieved only by a craftsman skilled in that field of work. It was the kind of finish that can be achieved only by a surgeon... or by a man adept at preserving bodies...'

'An undertaker...' muttered Cauvain.

'There is only one undertaker in this area, and he is presently sub-contracted by Bishop Montague – the bishop responsible for the building of the Sacré-Coeur. This man is responsible for the grandest Catholic funerals this side of the city, so he would be both a craftsman with a scalpel and with a hammer and nail.'

'And you propose we pay him a visit, Doctor?'

I tapped my pocket. 'That is why I suggested we arm ourselves... Come.'

An autumnal mist had descended with the coming of the night and, as Cauvain and I raced through the streets, my mind was thrown back to some of our escapades in London, Watson.

We reached a small cottage standing alone on the edge of the vast expanse of Montmartre Cemetery. The graveyard was unlit so beyond the first few tombstones was nothing but an inky blackness. The light from the cottage shone like a blazing beacon.

We pushed against the front door and were surprised to find it was not locked. We stepped into a small, dimly-lit parlour. Wooden coffin lids of all sizes leaned against the bare stone walls, the smell of polish enough to stifle one's breathing.

'Who is it?' It was the voice of an old man, coming from deeper inside the house.

'Monsieur Saint-André…?' There was nought but silence. 'We have come to talk to you about the deaths of Claude Giannini and the dogs of Montmartre…'

Hearing nothing, I thought for a moment that the fellow may have made his escape. Cauvain and I ventured forward towards an internal door that creaked as we pushed it open and treaded cautiously into a workshop. 'Monsieur Saint-André…?'

'Are you the police?' It was a tiny gentleman with a wizened face, wearing an apron that looked like it had never been washed. He had kind, doleful eyes and a thick white brush of a moustache on his lip.

Saint-André held out both hands as if submitting to an arrest. 'Please take me away, messieurs. I admit full responsibility for my actions and I can only beg God to forgive me…'

Cauvain and I were both wrong-footed by this poor little character who looked like a shoemaker from a fairy story.

'I am Inspector Lestrade of the Paris Police Prefecture,' I lied, recalling our favourite inspector from Scotland Yard! 'And this is my assistant… We would like to ask you some questions.'

Minutes later, poor Saint-André had boiled a saucepan of water and was brewing us tea. If this had been a real arrest, it would have been the most congenial ever endured. He slowly explained the strange assignments he had been given in the past week.

'My orders have come through a messenger boy on each occasion,' he elucidated. 'For each dog, I was asked to prepare a crucifix, which I assembled in this workshop before the dead beasts were brought in. But then, for poor Giannini, a more rigorous use of my craft was required, stitching the mortal wound across his throat, then preparing and setting the boy's body in that strange position. It was a gruelling and grisly business, and one I hope never to repeat. He was taken away by my usual runners – they would not have known what was inside the box – then delivered to the basilica where he was put on the cross…'

'Where did these orders come from?' Cauvain interjected.

'I was never given a name, sir, but the messages had the seal of one of the highest Catholic orders in this city. And they urged me to diligently but discreetly carry out my tasks, for I was carrying out what they called, "the unpleasant but wholly necessary work of God."' The undertaker crossed himself. 'I pray I am not betraying that highest power by speaking to you, gentlemen. But what they did-… what I was ordered to do to Giannini, it disgusted me… I now feel I must confess my sins if I am then to renounce them.'

I was about to press him for more information when there came a loud thump on the door. We all three froze, fearing we had been located by whatever higher forces had been controlling Saint-André.

'Messenger boy!' came a youthful cry.

I nodded at the old man, and so he went to the door with a casual air. Once the boy had left, the undertaker handed me the envelope, sealed with red wax. Upon the wax was a simple symbol of a cross with two hands clasped below it.

I thumbed it open and read the short hand-written note:

The next soul to be sacrificed to our Lord for his sins shall arrive by midnight. Your work must be completed by dawn tomorrow when the body will be collected. May God be with you.

Underneath the message was a crude diagram, of a man suspended upside-down, his feet bound together, and his arms stretched out – an inverted crucifixion. But it was the structure from which the man was being dangled that immediately caught our attention, badly drawn but unmistakeable...

It was the Eiffel Tower.

IV. The Race to the Tower

Cauvain and I burst out of Saint-André's cottage workshop. I caught up with the messenger boy who was climbing into a waiting horse-drawn taxi cab. I grabbed the poor wretch and asked him who had given him the message and where he was when he received it. He was happy to share what he knew for a small fee. I ordered him to get another ride home and threw him some additional centimes for the fare.

Cauvain hopped into the cab beside me. I shouted the address the boy had provided to our driver.

It was over three miles to our destination: an expensive, cosily-lit restaurant nestled into the stony bank of the Seine. Thick fog rose from the great river's still, black waters. Only the sweeping gaslight at the apex of the Eiffel Tower guided our driver through the darkness.

The great steel structure loomed high above the door of the restaurant. How apt, I thought, given our mission. We entered the establishment at speed, surprising the maître d'. He screamed at us to enquire if we had made a reservation, but we ignored him and instead scanned the room for our quarry.

Well-to-do diners looked up from their cordon bleu feasts to ascertain the commotion caused by us plainly-dressed intruders.

A short elderly man with close-cropped hair and a neat dark-grey beard sat alone in the far corner, sipping onion soup from a spoon. I recognised him instantly from the Paris newspapers, and at once I realised he was the man we were here to save. I approached his table with purpose, inadvertently nudging other customers on my way.

The man was startled to see I had come to address him. 'Monsieur!' I bellowed. 'We are here because you are in mortal danger!'

It was the engineer responsible for the tower outside and one of the most famous men in France…

It was Gustave Eiffel.

'What is the meaning of this intrusion, sir?' Eiffel demanded, standing to attention. He unbuttoned the top of his waistcoat, as if expecting to be drawn into a fistfight.

Breathlessly, I explained the events that had led us there. The messenger boy had informed me that he had been sent to Saint-André's workshop by a priest outside this very restaurant, so one could assume that the chosen victim was dining inside. The killer would be waiting to pounce on Eiffel before sending his dead body to be prepared by the undertaker in Montmartre. By dawn, the engineer would be cruelly suspended from his most famous creation, a gruesomely ironic statement that would forever sully the public perception of the Eiffel Tower.

'But why? Why would anyone do this?!' begged Eiffel.

Cauvain hobbled to my side. 'Modernity, sir,' he announced. 'Your tower symbolises everything certain factions of the Church despise. Progress, liberalism — you and your work, different political ideas, art, other cultures... There are some who view those concepts as something to fear, as a threat to their hold on power and on the morality of this city's population.'

Eiffel and, indeed, the restaurant's entire clientele went stony silent, Cauvain's words filling the air. Paris was the epicentre of a cultural revolution — one that challenged the old to accept the new. Not everyone was comfortable with that thought.

The thick quietness was rudely broken by the front door swinging open as violently as it had when Cauvain and I arrived.

It was Inspector Diomede of the Paris police again, accompanied by his two constables. A look of surprise flickered across his face when he registered me. 'Ah, it seems we've been beaten to the scene once more,' he smiled. 'You seem to possess some kind of sixth sense, Doctor — or, perhaps, you are more closely connected to these crimes than I first thought?'

I nodded contritely at the inspector who was as bullish and self-important as our friends from Scotland Yard. I detected he was merely vocalising the blow to his pride at being a step behind me, more than he were planning to arrest me.

Diomede continued: 'Monsieur Eiffel, we are here to protect you as we fear there may be an attempt made on your life tonight.' The policeman turned to me and Cauvain. 'We can take it from here, thank-you, gentlemen.'

I still had reason to feel concerned for Gustave Eiffel's personal safety, but the two burly constables prised their weighty frames past us and frogmarched the famous engineer towards the door of the building. Once the police and Eiffel had disappeared out into the night, the professor and I were left standing redundantly in the middle of the restaurant floor. The diners tutted indignantly at us and returned to their meals, unaware that the adventure had not yet come to an end.

The fog was even denser than earlier when we re-emerged onto the paved thoroughfare along the Seine. Cauvain spotted a cluster of shadows in the distance but suddenly they were gone, swallowed up by the murky whiteness. Again, the light at the top of the Eiffel Tower served as our saviour. 'Diomede must be escorting Eiffel to his private apartment,' cried the professor. 'It's at the top of the tower.'

As we neared the northern foot of the tower, we hit pockets where the fog cleared for a moment. Flashes of Diomede's party came into view, Gustave Eiffel among them. Cauvain took a breath to shout to them, but I placed the back of my hand on his chest to stop him.

At the base of the tower furthest south, I caught a glimpse of a single figure – a man, hooded, wearing a long robe.

'Doctor, over there!' exclaimed Cauvain in a whisper… He had seen, to our left, another figure silhouetted in the half-light, also dressed in a long robe.

I looked to the right and, for the briefest moment, a third such figure appeared.

'Are they priests…?' asked Cauvain quietly. 'Or monks…?'

I could not identify them, but they were an eerie sight, indeed. Cloaked by fog once more, we held our position. Tantalising images of the robed men flashed into view only to disappear just as suddenly. Each time we spotted them, they had moved a few paces. They were slowly closing in on Eiffel, Diomede and the police...

It was time to move. Cauvain followed my lead.

When we reached the wide space beneath the main shaft of the Eiffel Tower, the fog seemed to dissipate. We were stood between the edifice's four great iron feet. Eiffel, Diomede and the policemen were just a few yards away from us... And the pursuers in long robes circled us all. 'Halt!' rang out a voice from under a hood.

Diomede and his group stopped in unison. 'Who's there? Identify yourselves.' shouted the inspector impatiently.

One of the robed men removed his hood. A tanned face with black and grey hair appeared. It was the priest from Blanchard's establishment, who had also followed us to Salima Perez's home.

'We have come for Monsieur Eiffel, Inspector,' the priest declared confidently. 'I must ask you to hand him over to us...'

Diomede was in no mood to compromise. He pulled out a standard police revolver and raised it up in the direction of the priest. 'I will not give him up, sir,' the policeman announced with a tone of stubborn determination.

At that moment, Diomede noticed the presence of Cauvain and myself. He gave me the hint of a nod.

'Please, Inspector Diomede,' the priest persisted. 'We serve a greater good… a greater cause than yours. You must give us Gustave Eiffel.'

The elderly engineer was still in rude health and yet he cowered to a stoop when he realised the men around him were bartering for his very life. He took a position just behind Diomede.

The other two hooded men who had remained silent up to this point approached stealthily but steadily. With chilling synchronisation, they both pulled out pistols of their own – one had his weapon trained on Diomede, and the other on Eiffel behind.

Cauvain glanced at me, desperately seeking an order to advance. He fingered his gun. I raised my hand to stop any sudden moves from him.

'Do you know what signal it will send if Eiffel is suspended, dead, from his own tower…?' It was the priest, closing slowly on the inspector.

'Yes, I do,' Diomede retorted. 'It will mean fear once again etched into the hearts of all Parisians… Fear of God. Fear of change. Fear of the Church. The greatest demonstration of religion's power over our society…'

Diomede's finger twitched on his gun. He knew he was surrounded but he also knew one pull of the trigger would end the life of this mysterious priest.

I noticed the inspector whispering something to his two constables. Up to this point, I had taken them both to be unarmed other than the truncheons dangling impotently from their belts. Yet, with clinical swiftness, the two of them pulled out pistols from inside their tunics, and, without warning, shot at the two hooded predators on each flank. The robed men both dived for cover, retreating into the fog.

Only the silver-haired priest now remained.

'You will regret this,' cried the clergyman, his voice quivering with anger as the gunshots still rang in our ears.

'I feel little remorse, sir,' said Inspector Diomede.

He slowly squeezed on the trigger, ready to rid the world of this priest.

But the split-second before Diomede could take fire, a small lead bullet smashed into the side of his cranium, his skull imploding and his brain pierced instantly. The police inspector slumped to the floor with not even a cry.

Cauvain looked at me incredulously. I was holding my revolver, sulphurous smoke swirling into the fog around us. 'You-... You shot him?!' exclaimed the professor, staring at me as though I may turn on him.

I shot at the first constable who was frozen in shock, the bullet scraping his shoulder. I managed to blast a bullet through the right hand of the other constable, sending his own weapon spinning onto the pavestones. Both held up their hands in instant surrender and backed away from the body of their superior.

'I have no quarrel with you, constables – only with your Inspector Diomede,' I explained. Cauvain still looked at me as if I were the devil himself.

Gustave Eiffel slumped to his knees, ready to accept his inevitable fate.

'Monsieur Eiffel – it is alright,' said the priest calmly, stepping towards the engineer. He pulled Eiffel up by the hand. 'I and my brothers were here to protect you…' The priest and then Eiffel looked at me as I approached them. 'Though it seems we need not have worried with this man here to defend you.'

I shook hands with the priest. 'Our Lord will be most grateful to you, Doctor,' he smiled. 'As will Bishop Montague.'

Cauvain's stunned expression demanded I explain what had occurred.

'It is quite alright, Professor,' I reassured him. 'The killing is over.'

I told him how I had suspected Inspector Diomede of close links with the Church when he loaned me his knife in order to pull a nail from the crucifix up at Sacré-Coeur. The ornate engraving on the inspector's ivory-handled knife was of two hands clasped in brotherhood, with a cross above them – the symbol of the Order of Friars Minor, commonly known as the Franciscans.

'The same as on the wax seal on the letter to Saint-André the undertaker,' remembered Cauvain.

'Quite right,' I replied. 'Except the engraving on the knife also included an inscription: *MXXLII*.'

Cauvain added the Roman numerals in his head: '1252? What is the meaning of that?'

'1252 was the year,' I elucidated, 'when the Franciscans were approved to use torture and even execution against any presumed heretic, at the order of the pope. They were official inquisitors.'

'The Inquisition... A most shameful time for our faith,' the priest elaborated.

I continued my explanation: 'The blade confirmed my suspicions – a scalpel-style but I noticed the metal on the knife had a small kink in it. That kink was evident in the wounds on Giannini's body – you will recall, Cauvain, those strange blotches dotted across his cut throat. Not even Saint-André's handiwork could conceal them.'

'Brilliant, Doctor,' said the priest.

'Then, who are you?' Cauvain asked the cleric.

'My apologies – I should have introduced myself sooner,' he said. 'I am Father Gregory of the Franciscan Order, but – I am pleased to say – not connected to Diomede's strange and bloodthirsty sect. His selfish actions could have spelt the end of our Order. We would never have recovered from the shame. I followed you both when I felt you were onto something – our investigations were one and the same. I had not worked out the links between the victims, but then realised you may have done just that. My apologies if I frightened you both.'

Gustave Eiffel finally found his voice: 'Why did Diomede want me dead?'

'For those reasons he said before he was shot,' Gregory elaborated. 'Diomede and his kind rue the loss of the Catholic Church's power in this country. He resisted change – political and cultural. By making public sacrifices of those that his breed of Catholic detests – artist, revolutionary, those of other faiths – he hoped to put an end to such practices. At first, he used the dogs as warnings, all belonging to widows of those he felt had betrayed France. A cowardly act. But when the young artist Giannini painted something he took to be blasphemous, he took more direct action against him, and he had in place plans to continue the killing – starting with you, Monsieur Eiffel.'

Gustave Eiffel looked up at the shaft of the structure above.

'Only they were beliefs *he* upheld, not me,' continued Gregory. 'Nor most of us in the Church. We must embrace the time in which we live. We cannot stop the world from turning.'

'I knew this tower had caused some fissures within polite society, pitting conservative against progressive,' Eiffel whimpered, 'but I never expected it to provoke murder. Especially not my own!'

A week later, I was back at Monsieur Ferri's, sharing my usual table with Renard, Maurier, and my dear friend Professor Maximilian Cauvain. The two old men knew nothing of our adventures but excitedly gobbled up the rather sensationally reported accounts in the newspapers. The press had reported Diomede's shame, but concluded that other members of the Parisian force had uncovered his plot and shot him dead in battle at the Eiffel Tower.

This suited both Cauvain and me, as well as Father Gregory, I'm sure.

Diomede had kept on his person a list of his proposed victims. It was a list that included some of the most prominent and influential scientists and artists within French society.

In the days following our adventure, I had spent many hours with the new prefect of the Paris Police, a Louis Lépine. In fact, while in his company, I shared some of my knowledge of forensic science – he himself a keen advocate of such methods and a progressive in terms of criminal investigation.

My adventures had reignited a spark within me, Watson, though I knew it was still too soon to return to London. I became nervous that my success in bringing down Diomede's plot may attract some attention from the criminal fraternity. I needed to remain incognito and so knew it was time for me to leave Paris and to head south.

I shook hands with my companions and heaved my hefty kitbag onto my shoulder. Renard was in most splendid spirits – his interview with Madame Poesy the flower-seller had led to some more sociable meetings between the two of them in the days since. I wished both him and Maurier well. They continued to grumble about the changes in the city and yet they were a decent enough pair.

Cauvain accompanied me outside and stood with me while I waited to attract a passing cab. 'I can't thank you enough, my friend, for everything you've done for me,' he smiled warmly. 'And, of course, for preserving the secret from my past… You know, I still marvel at how you foiled Diomede's plot…'

I shook his hand as a horse-drawn carriage pulled up beside us. '*C'est élémentaire, professeur. C'est élémentaire...*'

'*Au revoir,*' said Professor Cauvain from the pavement as I settled in to my seat. I confess, though, Watson, that Cauvain's last farewell rather startled me: '*Bon voyage...* Mister Holmes.'

The Curse of the Baskervilles

Covering Note to *The Curse of the Baskervilles*

"Look not mournfully into the past, it comes not back again. Wisely improve the present, it is thine. Go forth to meet the shadowy future without fear and with a manly heart."

Henry Wadsworth Longfellow, *Hyperion* (1839)

I think of this quotation by that esteemed American writer regularly whilst chronicling the exploits I have shared with Mr Sherlock Holmes. Contrary to my friend's opinion, I am a reluctant scribe, though I feel I bear a singular responsibility to share with the public at large Holmes's peculiar but brilliant methods of deduction. This responsibility continually requires my looking back into the recent past, though I would proffer this is only so that we can better meet our future – "with a manly heart," if you will – having learned from history.

There was one occasion, though, when Longfellow's words echoed in my mind even as the mystery unfolded, like a chilling portent against our re-visiting of old adventures.

When, famously, we first encountered the family in question in this story, I feared we may come face-to-face with a monstrous beast sent by the Devil himself. In truth, our foe was but a human one, though no less dangerous in his intent to destroy an English ancestral line and all that crossed his path. Those events have been shared in *The Strand* and, in spite of being one of our more macabre adventures, the satisfyingly earthly conclusion proved palatable for modern audiences and even gained a certain notoriety in literary circles.

When Holmes and I were drawn into a case that echoed that celebrated tale, again involving the same dynasty, there felt to me something unsettling, as if one should never endeavour to challenge providence for a second time.

'Look not mournfully into the past…'

I wish I had taken heed of Longfellow's advice. Certain elements within this account haunt me to this day and so I only hope that by committing them to paper, I shall rid them of some of their ghoulishness, though I confess to writing with unsteady hand and pounding heart as I think of our journey back into the lives of that most cursed and unfortunate family that is the Baskervilles.

John H. Watson, M.D.
24th October 1910

I. One Word: Baskerville

Despite a chill wind and a fresh flurry of snow, the streets around London were abuzz with seasonal gaiety. The clocks had yet to strike four, but day was already turning to night, the sky ablaze in a strange dark orange and purple hue. The theatres around the West End and Piccadilly were churning out smiling families who had enjoyed the wholesome entertainment of the pantomime matinees, soon to be replaced with grown-up revellers eager for the less salubrious fare of the music-hall revues.

Perhaps it was this merry fever of festivity that compelled me to find a quiet place in which I could gather my thoughts before returning home to Baker Street. I confess that Christmas-time and, worse still, that period between December the twenty-fifth and the coming of the new year, had taken on a maudlin form in recent years. Sherlock Holmes was a fine friend and, by and large, a most amenable living companion – however, during this week on the calendar, he would skulk and sulk around our rooms like a caged lion, restless and irritable. Then, every year, without warning, he would bolt from his chair and petulantly exclaim he was to find stimulation elsewhere, as if his crotchety mood were all my creation. During that Yuletide of 1900, Holmes's will snapped just after Boxing Day, leaving me alone at the very time relatives and friends would traditionally while away the short winter days feasting and enjoying one another's company.

It was now New Year's Eve and I had eagerly volunteered to take on calls throughout the past few days, receiving plaudits for allowing my colleagues with wives and families to spend time at home. In truth, I was glad to be busy and away from my empty rooms.

My rounds completed, I dodged the revellers and the roaring braziers of the chestnut-sellers and slipped into a welcoming door in which I could find respite from the crowds. I realised I was in the famous Long Bar at the Criterion. It was too late for lunch and too early for dinner, so I was content to order a warming brandy while taking in the day's papers, perching myself on a stool by the spectacular gold and mosaic walls that reflected merrily on the dark liquid in my glass.

I looked around for any members of the club I might know – I was not an associate, but I knew many fellow medicos were – but imagined they would all be too occupied with family to find themselves here at this time.

I realised I was sitting in the very place my old colleague Stamford found me when I was at such an impasse in life following my discharge from the army. It suddenly struck me, as I breathed in the aroma of fresh varnish and observed the leather armchairs that it would soon be exactly twenty years since that chance encounter; an encounter which led directly to my introduction to Sherlock Holmes!

Strange, I thought, that I had never turned into the Criterion since, and yet chance – and my rather anti-social disposition – had impelled me to enter its doors, seemingly unconsciously, so close to that significant anniversary.

The soothing drink and the cosy warmth of the oil lamps around lifted my spirits a little and, after a half an hour, I felt ready again to face the cold and return to Baker Street.

I had barely seen Holmes since his outburst four days prior, for he would only emerge from his chambers each night after dark and return at an ungodly hour, if he returned at all. I knew never to question his whereabouts or his habits, but rather assumed they involved some kind of devilment, possibly with some of the more wretched characters in London society. With no cases landing at our door, as was almost always the way around Christmas, Holmes was cursed with a compulsion to seek out danger for himself.

Perhaps cheered by my drink, I resolved to treat my friend to dinner at Marcini's should I catch him back home. It was time for us both to re-join the rest of the world, to ring in the new year together and to mark our two decades of friendship.

I settled my bill and asked a young steward to collect my topcoat and medical bag from the cloakroom.

When the lad returned with my things, he also carried a small envelope which he presented to me. 'Dr Watson?' he checked.

I nodded uncertainly – nobody knew I was here – and saw that my name was written on the front. I opened it and pulled out a notelet.

Written upon it was one word. A name. A name that provoked a shudder of fear as I read it…

Baskerville

'Where did this come from?' I asked, flustered.

'Upstairs, sir. In the club,' the steward replied. 'The sender has invited you to join them, if you would care to follow me.'

Without thought, I was climbing the staircase and entering an antechamber off the main club rooms. The steward gestured towards a tall booth in the otherwise empty space.

'Thank-you, Hicks,' came a voice from the booth, and the boy left. It was a female voice.

I sidled onto a leather bench-seat at the table. 'How did you know I was here. Miss-…?'

'Miss Catrin Meredith,' she smiled sweetly, giving me her hand. She was a most radiant young woman, in her mid-twenties, tousled dark-brown hair gathered under a neat box-hat and wearing a suit of purple silk above pristine-white cotton blouse. Her freckles around her neat button nose gave her a youthful air, and yet she bore an elegance that only came with age. 'I trust I haven't alarmed you, Doctor. I am ashamed to say I have followed you most of this day, sir.'

'Followed me?'

'Yes, from Baker Street this morning through to now. I have been most eager to garner your attention.' She strived for a gentrified accent associated with one of high society, but her sing-song intonation was unmistakeably Welsh, and, I felt, all the more pleasant for it.

'Since this morning?' I spluttered.

'When I saw how busy you were – on your rounds – I felt it better to wait until you had finished,' she said. 'Such important work should not be disturbed.'

Her politeness was almost disarming. I had rarely met someone so unassumingly beautiful.

'I rather hoped to speak to both you and Mr Sherlock Holmes, but I notice he is absent from your rooms also,' she said. I smiled inwardly as I expected he had slumbered through any knocks on the door, sleeping off the vices of the previous night.

'You mention Baskerville in your note, Miss Meredith.'

'Yes, Dr Watson. I thought that name might interest you.'

'It most certainly does, Miss,' I laughed mirthlessly. 'What is it you want to tell me?'

Catrin Meredith fingered the edges of her skirts nervously, almost too frightened to elaborate. 'It's my sister, Dr Watson,' her voice quivered. 'I fear she's in the gravest danger. Her fiancé died just the day before Christmas, sir. A lovely boy, he was. Elis Williams he was called. Innocent, but not stupid, not prone to impulsive acts... Driven to his death, they're saying...'

Her voice cut as she recalled the sorry tale. I reached for my medicine bag in case she should need some smelling salts to calm her, but she composed herself.

'He went mad, Doctor – he suddenly started screaming and ran from the house where he worked, out into the hills in the middle of a fierce snowstorm. He was found dead the next morning ...'

I tried to reassure her while she caught her breath.

She continued valiantly: 'Elis was a servant in a country manor in the middle of Wales, not far from the border with England. Near where I come from...' She paused for a moment. 'On that night, sounds were heard. Strange sounds in the house and strange sounds outside on the hills. I wouldn't usually take any notice of such things, but the other servants heard this voice – a little girl's voice – and it was calling his name. This girl was calling for Elis...'

'It could be anyone,' I offered. 'Are there children in the house?'

'No, sir,' she replied. 'Not anymore. You see, it used to be an orphanage until one of the orphans – a little girl – died a couple of years ago. Influenza, Doctor – a terrible thing. The other orphans were sent away should they fall to the same illness, and the orphanage shut forever.'

'So, what are you saying?' I asked. 'You think Elis was being contacted by the spirit of the dead girl?'

'I don't know what to think, Doctor,' she said. 'I'd probably be as doubtful as you – I've been away for so long now, working here in London, and yet there was something else...'

'What? What else, Miss Meredith?'

'Another sound... heard for miles around when Elis was lost in the storm...'

I waited as she wiped a frightened tear away from her eye.

'It was the sound of a hound, Doctor...'

'And what of it?' I asked.

'It was said the baying of this hound could wake the dead!' she whimpered. 'And when they found Elis's body the next morning, he bore the wounds of a man who had been savaged – savaged by a dog it seems, but its bite-marks larger than anything native to these shores.'

I shuddered as I recalled our famous adventures in Dartmoor some years earlier. I shuddered even more when Catrin Meredith concluded her story.

'The house where Elis worked – well, it's owned owned by a particular family. A family you know all too well, Doctor…'

I finished her sentence for her. 'The Baskervilles…'

'You know it's customary for one to give the gift of china on a twentieth anniversary, Watson,' Sherlock Holmes smiled as he met me at the doors of the Criterion. I was rather flattered that he had remembered the significance of the venue and the upcoming anniversary.

The prospect of a mystery to solve had put my friend in the most cheerful of spirits. An hour earlier, I had got a message to Holmes from the club, with the poor messenger boy promised an extra crown should he manage to wake him! Holmes had even been amused by my cheek in suggesting the messenger should request the extra payment from the recipient himself. He had been happy to do so after reading my message:

"The game is afoot! We have an intriguing case. Criterion immediately."

Catrin Meredith explained to the two of us over dinner that she had moved to London when she was sixteen in order to pursue a career on the stage. She had flourished in the West End, making a decent living with her acting and prodigious singing voice, initially in the music halls and then as a serious actress taking on some of the most challenging female roles in theatre. Her most recent turn had been as Desdemona in a triumphant production of *Othello* at the Theatre Royal on Drury Lane.

Holmes realised he had seen her perform two winters previously in Oscar Wilde's great new tragedy, *Salomé*. She had built a reputation as a thespian who performed in a truthful, contemporary style, and was much in demand with the city's most respected impresarios.

For all the glamour of her present life, she had grown up in Montgomeryshire, a most rural county that stretches almost across the whole breadth of Wales just above its middle. It is a wild, verdant terrain cradling tumbling hills, craggy banks and roaring rivers. The deaths of Catrin's parents meant her younger sister, Teleri, was her only remaining family. Teleri stayed in the area and the sisters remained very close, writing to one another each week.

'Dear Teleri also has acting ambitions and so loves to hear my stories from the theatre,' Catrin Meredith reported. 'She hopes someday to join me here and to tread the boards though

I fear it is not an easy profession in which to succeed and have advised her to make her life nearer home. I had hoped that her union with Elis would keep her in Wales, as I confess myself to struggling most desperately when I first arrived in London and would not wish her to experience the same hardship.'

Teleri, aged twenty-one, had been courting Elis for two years and the two were committed to marry. Catrin had visited them on frequent occasions and approved wholeheartedly of the match.

Elis had grown up at Baskerville Court and worked there as a servant until his demise. The country manor, nestled in a wide valley, was used as an orphanage for many years and Elis was housed there after both his parents perished in south Wales.

Baskerville Court was the property of the Baskerville-Wilkes family. On the broadest family tree, the Baskerville-Wilkes line would be three columns across from the Baskervilles of Dartmoor whom Holmes and I encountered in our earlier adventures.

Wilfred Baskerville-Wilkes was head of the family. He had made his colossal fortune through coal in the south Wales valleys. His coal-mines stretched across most of Glamorgan, fuelling homes and industries throughout Britain and, indeed, throughout her Empire. Wilfred was a rich man, but also much-loved. He was a philanthropist who had turned the family home in Montgomeryshire into an orphanage for parentless children from the industrial south, Elis among them.

Wilfred had spent the past decade in Canada, prospecting for coal and, by all accounts, increasing his fortune tenfold. Still, though, he did not forget the orphans at the Court and he would regularly send donations for refurbishments to the house or to help its former residents who had grown into adulthood.

'Responsibility for Baskerville Court was bestowed upon Wilfred's son, Garfield Baskerville-Wilkes,' reported Catrin. 'Garfield was no older than forty, and seemed determined to display even greater benevolence than his much-loved father. Garfield funded a number of resources for the wider community including a new school hall and the preservation of the local chapel. A fine Christian gentleman…'

Catrin's visage changed as she continued. 'But tragedy struck Baskerville Court two years ago. The influenza that affected so many people across the country visited the orphanage. The life of a ten-year-old girl, Mabel Saunders, was claimed by the illness. Quickly, Garfield arranged for the other orphans to be placed elsewhere before any of them succumbed to the 'flu themselves.'

The dark episode had an effect on everyone in the farms and villages around with people heartbroken to see the popular Garfield plunge into a most bleak depression.

Catrin went on: 'My family – my parents, Teleri and me – we lived five miles away, which in that desolate area, made us neighbours to Garfield and the orphans at the Court, though our farmhouse was decidedly more humble. He is a most decent man, and even paid for my mother and father's burials last year.'

'My condolences, Miss Meredith,' said Holmes gently. 'And you returned home for their funerals?'

'One funeral, actually – for my parents died in the very same month and were laid to rest together. First, my mother from an infection, and then my father from a broken heart not a fortnight after. Shamefully, my employers would not release me to attend the funeral as I was contracted to play eight shows a week at the new Wyndham's Theatre and there was no understudy.'

It was clear the regret still pained her.

Holmes pressed his fingertips together as he considered the story. 'There is one thing I don't understand,' he said, 'and that is why you believe your sister Teleri to be in danger specifically.'

During our whole conversation, Catrin had barely touched her food, but now she set her knife and fork together on the side of the plate, conceding she would not eat another thing. 'Baskerville Court is said to be haunted, sirs. The night of Elis's death was not the first time the voice of poor little Mabel Saunders was heard in those corridors… It happened once before, when the name of the faithful house matron was uttered from thin air. Within days, that matron, who had cared for the orphans for many years, was found dead at the bottom of a nearby rockface. The stony path had crumbled beneath her on her walk to chapel…'

'A coincidence, I should imagine, Miss,' I offered.

'And then, since Christmas Day this past week, Teleri reports to me in a telegram received yesterday that her name is now being called every night by that same spectral voice… I don't consider myself superstitious, gentlemen, but they say that to be called by poor little Mabel is to be called to your death…'

II. Hounds in the Hills

It was a five-hour journey from London to Welshpool, cutting through the Midlands and the Black Country before crossing the border into Wales.

A dusting of snow was evident in the low-lying areas on our trip, though it thickened considerably as we reached the Welsh hills.

Holmes had gladly agreed to take on Catrin Meredith's case, though her theatrical commitments prevented her from joining us. Although familiar with the adage that the show's the thing, it seemed to me a savagely unsentimental business that places the needs of the audience always above the needs of the players, even in the most trying personal circumstances. I thought back to Catrin's evident remorse at missing the funeral of her own parents.

My additional duties over Christmas had allowed me to take a week's sabbatical in lieu and so I relished the opportunity for an expedition away from town. Twenty years since making one another's acquaintance, Sherlock Holmes and I were setting off on a new adventure, as if ourselves two decades younger.

I confess, though, to a nagging sense of dread. We had faced down a most nefarious enemy once before, as well as supposedly supernatural forces, in the aid of the Baskerville clan, and so I felt an unease at returning to another Baskerville estate, especially if the stories of young Elis being savaged by a beast bore any truth.

Soon we arrived in the amiable market town of Welshpool. Waiting at the platform was Catrin's sister, Teleri Meredith, instantly recognisable with the same cluster of freckles around her delicate nose. She bore the grace of her sister but carried with her the air of a country maid, her clothes simple, skirt frayed and muddied at the hem.

She smiled bravely as she greeted us, the loss of her sweetheart still fresh.

'Mr Holmes. Dr Watson... It is a pleasure to welcome you, sirs.' She shook our hands and led us to an unpretentious two-horse carriage waiting outside the small station. 'I rather feared the weather would prevent you from arriving.'

She must have noticed my surprise at the basic design of our transport. 'Don't worry, Dr Watson,' she laughed. 'This is the best buggy to get us across country in the snow. Mr Baskerville-Wilkes – Garfield – wanted to send his, but I told him it would never make it.'

'This will do fine,' said Holmes, settling onto a hard bench seat. 'Where's the driver?'

Teleri smiled and pointed to herself. 'Garfield said the least he could do was provide men's coats and extra blankets, so they're under your seats,' she told us as she perched on the driver's stool and geed her horses onto the road.

Flakes of snow floated magically around us as we joined a narrow dirt track, the wheels skimming against the banks. I was put in mind of some Russian scene I had seen in paintings, our sturdy troika pressing on through the icy wilderness!

Before I could begin the conversation by offering my condolences at the loss of Elis Williams, Holmes cut in with an abrupt line of questions. 'So, Miss Meredith, I understand you are the focus of a cursed spirit?'

'I know what you're thinking – simple country folk believing in fairy stories – but yes, a voice, Mabel's voice, has been calling my name. Every night at midnight, ever since Christmas… Ever since Elis-…'

'And this same voice called for your fiancé?'

'Yes, sir,' she said, pausing for a moment as she steered the carriage around a tight bend. 'I would never believe in such things, but the house-… well, Baskerville Court has taken on a most dark and sinister temperament ever since Mabel died. It's become a strange place… A sad place.'

It occurred to me I had never heard of a house talked about in this way before – as if it possessed a spirit of its own, with its own moods and feelings.

'Your sister tells us you live nearby, Miss,' said Holmes.

'Yes, I live a few miles east, at my parents' farm, though I have been staying at the Court ever since Elis's passing. I look after the horses for Garfield, you see, so I'm a regular at the house, but Elis's death has hit poor Garfield terribly – just like when Mabel went – so I've stayed around to keep the place tidy and arrange things for Elis's funeral.'

'Is there other staff at the Court?' Holmes enquired.

'Two other servants, sir, and there was Lynwen, but she passed away last year.'

'Ah, yes!' exclaimed Holmes, a little too excitedly. 'The matron who fell to her death on her way to chapel? I understand Mabel's voice called out to her too.'

'Lynwen was a wonderful woman. She was nanny to Garfield when he was a boy, and then, when the orphans were moved into the house, she looked after them all. Auntie Lynwen, they called her – Elis still did until she died. When the children left, dear Lynwen stayed behind to nurse Garfield back to health. He was quite distraught for some time, you see.'

'I should like to speak with Mr Baskerville-Wilkes when we arrive,' said Holmes.

'He's very much looking forward to meeting you, Mr Holmes,' Teleri replied, pulling her scarf up in front of her face as we turned into the wind.

'And Elis…' Holmes continued. 'He was killed by a hound?'

Teleri was understandably slower to answer this question, pain etched on her face as she negotiated the terrain. 'Yes, Mr Holmes. He was driven mad by hearing Mabel – out of character, but understandable after Auntie Lynwen's death… He just ran out towards the hills, they said, in weather much like this. I was at my house so knew nothing of it until the following morning – Christmas morning… He was due to visit me at ten o'clock but didn't appear.' She stopped her story a moment, choked by the memory.

'It's alright, my dear,' I assured her. 'Perhaps, Holmes, we should continue our questioning once we have reached our destination.'

'No, it's quite alright, Doctor,' she said. 'In some ways, it's a comfort to finally talk about this – Garfield hasn't been of sound mind and so I've had scant opportunity to discuss it.'

As I looked across the white, desolate landscape, and thought of Teleri living alone at the home of her deceased parents, I pondered how lonely such a bucolic existence could be.

'I rode to Baskerville Court before lunchtime when I sensed something was wrong,' she told us. 'I saw what I thought was a dead calf – a dark body on the side of a hillock, lifeless and bloody...' She paused as she thought back to what must have been a horrifying sight. 'I approached-... It was the shoes I noticed first – it was a man, not a beast. And I recognised his boots... And then the hand – Elis lost part of a finger as a boy, half of the little finger on his left hand. Most people would barely notice it at first. But this was my Elis – I knew it was him as soon as I saw that finger, an inch shorter than the others... His body was savaged, chunks torn out of him – bitten clean open across his stomach, his neck... his face, only just recognisable.'

'I'm so sorry,' I muttered impotently.

'My Elis – killed in the most horrific fashion... I rode on towards Baskerville Court – and came across poor Garfield searching in the snow, digging with his hands. Desperate, he was. He was freezing, not even wearing a coat... I told him there was nothing more he could do, and got him back to the house.'

'And Elis's body was examined?' asked Holmes.

'Yes, the local constabulary and the coroner inspected him,' she confirmed. 'It was they who said the bite marks was from an animal too big to belong to a regular hound – not any dog you'd find in this country, at least.'

'And someone had heard this dog during the night of his death?' I asked. 'Your sister mentioned…'

'Yes, Dr Watson,' Teleri replied. 'Garfield heard it, as did the other servants. Some people in some of the villages around reported the sound also. Garfield, of course, thought immediately of the curse on his cousins in Dartmoor that you know all too well, sirs… He had never thought his line of the family to be struck with the same hex, and yet the noises terrified him.'

The afternoon sun was sinking low on the horizon. Darkness would soon fall, and the snow was coming down harder, whipping past us as we sped westward.

The strange muffled silence produced by a carpeting of snow was broken by a chilling noise, somewhere in the distance.

The howling of a pack of dogs…

I froze in my seat and shot a look at Holmes. Here we were again heading to a Baskerville estate, with the sound of beasts filling the air. My friend, as ever, seemed unperturbed. Even Teleri did not flinch.

'You've had a fox-hunt here today, Miss Meredith?' said Holmes in a matter-of-fact tone. 'The sound of pointers, spaniels and terriers, if I'm not mistaken... Nothing to be afraid of, Watson.'

'Yes, Lord Caradog owns all this land you can see around us. All the way to the boundary with Baskerville Court. He hosts a New Year's Day hunt, riders come from all over.'

'Were you part of the event, Teleri?' I asked. 'A fine horsewoman.'

'No, sir,' she smiled ruefully. 'Gentry only! Lord Caradog doesn't mix with us locals.' There was a trace of contempt in her voice. 'Caradog is the complete opposite to the Baskervilles – he thinks about nothing but adding to his property and to his wealth... He couldn't care less about anyone around here – my parents used to keep geese, and he shot the birds dead when they flew over his fields. He would dine on them all winter.'

'He sounds a contemptible sort,' I blustered.

'That's not the worst of it, though, Doctor,' said Teleri. 'Elis used to tell me how, five years ago, old Wilfred Baskerville-Wilkes – Garfield's father – sent the orphans in the house a most loveable pet all the way from Canada. A puppy, playful and strong-willed! Elis loved that animal – he had such a way with God's creatures – but then, after just six months, the beloved dog went missing in the hills and never came back. A week passed before Lord Caradog apparently informed Garfield that he had slain the animal as he feared for his livestock or cross-breeding with his pack of hunting dogs.

Elis was devastated, as you can imagine, being fifteen at the time and having never felt the love of a family.'

It struck me that for all the respect afforded this nation's aristocracy, a disproportionate number of them behaved brutishly and, as Holmes and I had often experienced first-hand, with the criminal intent one more typically associates with the working classes.

My line of thought was jarred by the appearance over the brow of a hill of a dozen hunting dogs, yapping desperately, bobbing and spinning around one another. Their barks were panicked, high-pitched, as if warning of a great danger but terrified of being heard. Something had driven them quite mad.

Teleri guided her horses onto the side of the slush-covered track, the back wheels of our buggy sliding for a moment before coming to an undignified stop.

'My apologies, sirs!' Teleri shouted to Holmes and me. The dogs shot across the path of the horses – had Teleri not stopped so quickly, we would have ploughed squarely into the hounds.

Two men appeared on horseback, silhouetted in the purple twilight, in pursuit of the dogs. The lead rider bellowed in our direction: 'Your horses must have scared my animals!'

Teleri sighed, unruffled by the incident. 'They did no such thing, Lord Caradog...' she rolled her eyes.

'They have been behaving erratically all day,' he whined in a singularly self-entitled tone. 'I knew one of you local peasants would be behind it. The hunt was spoiled, my guests left disappointed, and so I shall need to be recompensed for my embarrassment.'

Lord Caradog was younger than I expected, aged no more than two scores, with shaggy jet-black hair angled into neatly-trimmed sideburns. He wore a splendid crimson hunting jacket, unbuttoned, and beige jodhpurs tucked into mahogany-coloured riding boots, though he had dispensed with riding hat, presumably as the official hunt was long finished. He pulled his steed to a stop in front of our wagon, curious as to the identity of the passengers.

Behind him, the second rider slowed to a canter. His attire was purely functional, muddy riding boots and thick overcoat, and his dark, craggy face betrayed a life lived outside. 'Haydn,' Caradog addressed him. 'I'm tired of the chase – I woke up this morning dreaming of hunting the foxes, not the hounds.'

Haydn's face flashed the same world-weary look Teleri's had when she first saw Caradog. 'Very good, my lord,' he affirmed, before turning to Teleri. '*Swmae, Miss Meredith. Cofion cynnes i ti,*' he uttered in the local Welsh with a friendly smile before riding into the darkness, the yapping of hounds disappearing from earshot.

'I must ask, sir, that you clear the path and allow us to continue to Baskerville Court.' It was Holmes, irritated by the intrusion. 'I can assure you that, unless Miss Meredith here has the power to be in two places at once, she had no part in unsettling your hunting dogs – she has been with us for the entirety of this past hour.'

'And who, may I ask, would I be addressing?' Caradog scoffed pompously.

'My name is Mr Sherlock Holmes, and this is my companion, Dr Watson.'

Caradog hesitated a moment. I fancied he had read of our endeavours in the papers, for some of his bluster disappeared. 'A celebrity in our midst,' he confirmed my thinking, 'presumably come to look in on Garfield Baskerville-Wilkes… The man's insane, Mr Holmes. He should be put out of his misery and sent to an asylum.'

'And I suppose that will benefit you, will it not, Lord Caradog?' replied Holmes, a statement as much as a question. 'His estate backs onto yours, I believe?'

'I don't know what you might be suggesting, sir,' Caradog demurred, 'My family have lived here since before the English Civil War – I'm proud to say that they even sequestered some members of the Royal household away from the heathen Roundheads. We have a duty to preserve this land for the greater good. I only ask that my neighbours – gentry or commoner – control their animals and respect their boundaries.'

'Respect their boundaries?' Teleri cut in. 'Perhaps I should inform you that you have just crossed onto Mr Baskerville-Wilkes's land.' Caradog looked around him, confusion etched across his face. 'It seems that without Haydn to guide you, you're rather lost, Lord Caradog… Your house is three miles that way.' Teleri pointed north, while Caradog searched for a riposte that eluded him.

'Miss Meredith,' Holmes addressed our driver. 'Perhaps we should be getting into the warm – I fear another cold front coming in.'

Teleri snapped at the reins and away we went, Lord Caradog looking lost and frankly ridiculous, alone on his horse in the snow.

The sight of gaslight in the distance was a welcome one with a near-blizzard whipping at our faces. Baskerville Court was sited in a charming spot, nestled in a low valley, hills sloping up from its lawns.

Teleri had described it as a sad house and yet, as we approached, the driveway ribboning towards its front doors, it looked like a romantic scene from one of the Christmas cards that have recently become custom. Snow-covered roof, windows aglow with warmth, a shelter from the cold outside.

Teleri dropped us off by the front door. She asked us to wait until she had stabled her horses around the back. Baskerville Court was a splendidly-sized manor, small enough to be considered a house rather than the more palatial stately mansions that reek of money but little comfort. A navy-blue door was flanked by two horizontal rows of ten windows neatly dotted along its front. Vines crept up the walls, giving it a sense of it belonging to nature, as if the building had grown organically from the valley floor.

However, as we inspected it more closely in the half-light, Holmes and I could see that the paint on the window frames was peeling and there were tiles missing in the roof, smashed upon the floor where we stood. It was a place in need of some care. Indeed, the leafy creepers which lent it a fairy-tale feel were growing in and out of the stonework.

Holmes crouched down and picked up one of the sharp fragments of slate tile strewn on the ground. He continued to inspect the front of the house, his eyes focused on the floor as he trudged through the snow.

'What are you looking for, Holmes?' I asked, clapping my hands together for warmth. I hoped Teleri would be quick with the horses.

'It was just something I was thinking about in the carriage, Watson,' Holmes spoke in the off-hand manner he adopts when on a case. 'I fear, though, that the fresh snow may be our enemy here.'

I was about to enquire further when Teleri emerged from around a crumbling corner of the house. She took a deep breath. 'We should go in, gentlemen,' she said.

I could not place exactly what it was about Teleri's face that made me shudder as she led us to the front door… The way she said those words: '*We should go in…*' As if there was a reluctance on her part. Or possibly something more. Mournfulness, perhaps… Or was it fear?

III. Return of the Hound of the Baskervilles

'Welcome, Dr Watson!... And Mr Holmes!... Thank-you both for coming.' The welcome from Garfield Baskerville-Wilkes could not have been more convivial.

He had a round, ruddy face, and a body just on the plump side, and seemed a most merry fellow. He clasped my hand for many seconds before greeting Holmes in the same way.

'It is an honour, gentlemen,' he beamed. 'Teleri may have told you that I have read all of your marvellous accounts of your friend's work, Dr Watson.'

I did not know who was the more embarrassed – Holmes or myself – although I admit to enjoying Garfield's compliments.

'Thank-you, Mr Baskerville-Wilkes,' muttered Holmes.

'Mr Baskerville-Wilkes?!' spat our host cheerfully. 'Why, that's my father's name, not mine! Please, I insist you call me Garfield!'

Holmes looked decidedly awkward as Garfield patted him on his shoulder. For a moment, I thought he might pull my friend into an embrace!

'Now, where's Kitty?' Garfield asked, looking around the dimly-lit hallway. It struck me that there were few of the furnishings one would expect to find in an ancestral country home. The hall and stairs were carpeted but there were few trinkets or pictures on the wall – none besides a framed photograph at the top of the first flight of stairs. I could not make out the detail in the gloomy distance, though it looked like a school photograph.

'Coming, Garfield,' came a quiet voice. A young maid scuttled down the corridor. She ran to Teleri first, taking her hands for a moment in a greeting of touching solidarity. 'Kitty, it's good to see you,' Teleri smiled.

'And you, Miss,' Kitty replied. She would have been sixteen, but her blonde, almost cherubic, ringlets made her appear younger.

'Has he been alright?' Teleri gestured towards Garfield.

'The same,' Kitty replied. The master's state of health was clearly uppermost in the girls' thoughts.

'Kitty here will take your bags upstairs and show you to your rooms,' Garfield announced. 'I don't know what I'd do without her, I really don't,' he added, before turning to Teleri. 'And Teleri here- she's had the most awful loss, gentlemen. But she also remains a loyal friend to me. She has stayed here since poor Elis was taken from us. I do not deserve the care she and Kitty provide, but I am most grateful for it.'

He had an easy rapport with his servant and with Teleri which was rare, the polar opposite to Lord Caradog's more traditional treatment of his staff. I wondered if poor Haydn had managed to retrieve the dogs on the hills and get Caradog home.

Kitty took our lighter bags though I insisted Holmes and I carry our cases. The maid led us up the bleak stairway and to our bedrooms, Holmes and I staying next door to one another. 'You'll be in Elis's old room,' Kitty told me softly. The thought rather unsettled me at first, though I concluded it must be one of the few orphans' rooms still made up. It was strange to think, though, that the young man would have been sleeping in this very room just over a week previously. I dropped off my case and returned to the landing. A voice came from downstairs.

'Oh, Kitty!' It was Garfield. 'Did you lock the back entrance firmly? And check all windows?'

'Yes, sir, all double-checked as you request,' Kitty hollered back. She addressed Holmes and me: 'I'm afraid master Garfield has grown very unsettled these past few days. Paranoid, Teleri says... First Mabel's voice, then Elis's death at the jaws of-...'

The maid paused a moment, unable to articulate the words. *At the jaws of a hound...*

'He was good to me, gentlemen – Elis, I mean,' she mumbled.

'Are you local, Miss?' Holmes asked. 'Your accent suggests you hail from the Midlands – the Black Country, perhaps.'

'Moved into service from Wolverhampton, sir, not a year ago,' she said wistfully. 'Wanted a country placement – when you've grown up around the grime and the soot of the city, this place is like paradise... Well, it was, sirs. Until recently.'

A wind whistled through the upstairs landing where we stood. The two gas-lamps dotted along the corridor flickered for a moment before deciding to remain alight. 'I notice the place is in need of some maintenance,' I offered.

Holmes ran his hand along the sidewall, hovering it above the angle where the carpet hit the skirting board.

'Master Garfield seems reluctant to spend money on renovations,' Kitty told us. 'It's like he's lost his spirit.'

A sad house indeed, I thought.

We sat down for a meal of goose and trimmings. The cook did an excellent job, ably assisted by Kitty who ran back and forth from the kitchen with extra helpings. Teleri Meredith joined us at the table. Although she tended to his horses, Garfield clearly considered her more a neighbour and friend than an employee. She had stayed here this past week as his guest following Elis's death, and I imagine the master of the house was glad of the company. I have, in my past, treated some patients tormented by paranoia, often following a specific trauma. I could see in Garfield the familiar signs – his almost maniacal cheerfulness barely disguising his deeply-rooted nervousness. Living alone in this condition would be unsettling for the sufferer; even dangerous.

Garfield served us some excellent port which warmed up the atmosphere in the house. He was a man prone to more than just a glass or two, chugging back each measure in the time it took the rest of us to enjoy a slow sip. Another tell-tale sign of mania can be a reliance on alcohol.

'So, tell me, Garfield,' said Holmes, 'does your father return here regularly from Canada?'

'My father has not returned for some years, Mr Holmes,' Garfield responded between swigs. 'And, alas, I fear he will not return to Baskerville Court again…'

We remained silent while Garfield composed his thoughts. The colour rushed from his cheeks. 'Wilfred Baskerville-Wilkes is gravely ill, sirs,' he announced. 'A tumour in his lung… He was given just a few weeks to live, and that was some months past, so he is on borrowed time now. Indeed, every day, I expect the letter or wire to arrive that confirms his fate.'

I offered my condolences, though Holmes spoke over me. 'And you have no siblings?'

'No, Mr Holmes, I was not blessed with brothers and sisters, although I considered the orphans who passed through our home as family.'

'Do you stay in touch with the orphans, sir?' Holmes pressed on. Inwardly, I begged he would stop and continue his interrogation at a more appropriate time.

'With Elis, of course, who worked here,' Garfield spoke softly and with more than a trace of remorse. 'Others send occasional cards. My father's – and my – wishes were always that they would go on to live independent lives. I'm happy to say they all have.'

'It would please me to read some of their Christmas cards, Garfield – the orphans who have grown up and flourished,' Holmes said as he leaned back and began the ritual of filling his pipe with tobacco. 'I assume many sent their best wishes over this festive period?'

Teleri smiled expectantly. 'Oh yes, Garfield. It would be good to hear how well they are doing... and a comfort to me as my Elis spoke so warmly of them.'

Garfield considered the dark syrupy drops in his glass. 'I ordered that all remnants of Christmas be removed following the news of Elis. I will ask Kitty to check, but I fear they have been discarded already.'

Garfield leaned back in his chair and stared into nothingness for a few moments. Finally, the silence was broken. 'I would give anything... Anything to have those children back here again. It was a good home then. A happy one...'

I felt it was my Hippocratic duty to step in. The man was clearly disturbed and in no state to continue to answer Holmes's questions. 'I suggest we save the rest of this conversation for tomorrow. Garfield, Teleri — Holmes and I would very much like to see Elis's body in the morning.'

Teleri nodded affirmatively.

Kitty and the cook began to clear the dishes from the table, when Teleri suddenly froze. 'Quiet!' she said. The clatter of porcelain and silver continued for a moment, but then I heard it...

A howling!

'Quiet, everyone!' Teleri repeated.

We all held our positions like statues. The howling became louder.

'Caradog's hunting dogs?...' I whispered hopefully.

Holmes shook his head. A chill cut through my body.

The howling became even clearer now. Loud but deep and guttural. Like a demonic beast more than an earthly animal.

Between its loud calls, all one could hear was the fast breathing of the others around the table. The place was near-silent – each heartbeat, breath or gulp of air sounded as clear as a bell.

There were long gaps between howls, but all we could do in between was await the next canine cry.

Suddenly, there was a smash of glass. Kitty shrieked, but then realised it was Garfield Baskerville-Wilkes's port tumbler, shattered into a thousand pieces on the dining room's wooden floorboards. Garfield began to whimper. 'It's me it wants. It's my family curse…'

He rose from his seat and walked into the hallway. Before the rest of us could react, he was unlocking the front door. Another howl – this time, a gust of arctic wind – filled the house.

'It's me it wants!' Garfield cried.

As if mesmerised up to this moment, we all sprang into action, pursuing Garfield out of the door and into the thick snow.

The master of the house was fast. He was many yards up the drive already, not stopping for a coat or boots, gesturing to whatever beast was out there to come and claim him. 'Come on!... Take me!'

He collapsed to his knees and started clawing at the snow, digging with his hands and pulling it up in scoops. 'Take me!...'

Another howl filled the clear, star-filled sky above us. Deafening this time! It was close. The horses at the back of the house began to whinny in panic.

Then, all we heard was the heavy breathing of something giant. And then the snarling, snapping sound of a predator salivating, stalking its prey.

All around us was darkness, the black hills tumbling down towards the grounds of Baskerville Court, and yet a brilliant white half-moon allowed us to glimpse tantalising traces of detail: the flicker of a leafless tree bending in the wind, a half-broken gate sagging on its hinges, and then something moving… Something alive.

The dark, hulking shape of an animal, larger than any dog, its paws and legs thicker and stronger than a domestic pet, and its giant jaws capable of destroying anything that crossed its path.

It was a giant hound…

IV. A Call from the Dead

Garfield Baskerville-Wilkes swivelled around and saw the rest of the household assembled behind him.

'Get back, all of you!' he cried. 'This is my family's destiny!'

The shape of the hound was swallowed by the darkness. Still, though, we could hear it snorting expectantly, considering its next meal.

'You must come inside, sir!' I half-whispered, nervous my voice might attract the savage beast towards us. I turned to Teleri and Kitty who had followed us into the snow. 'Get back indoors, both of you…'

The two women seemed frozen to the spot for a few seconds, before walking backwards on their heels to the door.

Holmes remained as unflinching as the predator itself, his narrow eyes scouting the circumference of the grounds. I was relieved to see he carried his revolver.

Garfield Baskerville-Wilkes was a pathetic sight, still digging mindlessly at the snow. 'Come on, finish me off… This nightmare will be over then.'

A sudden movement, the solid crunch of snow under heavy paws, then-

Bang!

Holmes fired a second shot immediately after the first. There was a yelp of pain from the unseen beast and the sound of feet scrambling. With a last howl of dismay, the great animal raced off into the distance.

We stood in silence for a whole minute, finally assured that the beast had left. I approached Garfield. He was sobbing into the snow, his fingernails claggy with mud, ice and even blood where he had clawed too vigorously. I helped him up and led him inside.

Holmes surveyed the horizon for a little longer before following us in. I was grateful to hear Kitty lock the front door behind him once he was safely inside. I understood now why Garfield had been so paranoid about securing the doors and windows.

This beast was no regular dog like the original hound of the Baskervilles that Holmes and I encountered in Devon all those years ago.

I administered Garfield a sedative and, with Teleri's help, guided him to his bed. I hoped he would feel calmer in the morning. Holmes's shot had not killed the beast, though it was apparent it had been injured and so would be less of a danger to all around. Despite this logical thought, though, I still harboured a dark concern. What if this beast was supernatural, just as the original Baskerville curse had prophesised years before? Would its wounds be enough to quell its goal of destroying the Baskerville family? The rational side of my brain rallied against these fanciful and terrifying conjectures.

When Teleri and I descended the stairs, Holmes was inspecting the framed photograph I had noticed when we had arrived, holding a lantern up to the picture. It was a group of children, though it was not a school photograph as I had initially assumed.

'That's Elis just there,' Teleri indicated, pointing at a scrawny boy on the left of the group, his eyes dark and cheeks sallow. 'He was only ten then, just weeks after he'd arrived from Merthyr Tydfil. A godless place, he called Merthyr – a town forever beholden to the Crawshays' ironworks.'

'And the rest?' Holmes asked.

'The other orphans – ten of them at a time, there were.'

The children stood in front of the house, and although the image was tinged sepia and black, it was evident that the property was in far better condition back then, with flowers in the vines and a well-manicured garden fronting the well-kept house.

Holmes angled his lantern closer to the image. I could tell that something concerned him. 'A happy group?'

'Very, sir,' said Teleri. 'I remember some of them myself. I knew the ones my age in school and from chapel. All well looked after – look, there's Auntie Lynwen I told you about.'

Lynwen looked a sturdy, no-nonsense type, but there was a glint of a smile in her eyes, despite the staid and awkward pose so common in these Victorian portraits.

'And there's Garfield,' Teleri said, pointing at the much slimmer, younger version of our host. He had dispensed with the stuffy conventions of photography of the time and smiled broadly from ear to ear, like a proud father to these children around him. I thought about the disturbed figure sleeping upstairs and how situations beyond our own control can have such an effect on our mental faculties. Most of my medical colleagues called it insanity, but there was something dismissive in that term, as if the patient were either mad or not. I preferred to think of the brain as a changing organism that could have good days and bad, no different to gout or backache.

'And this girl...' Holmes ran his finger along the line of faces to a sad-looking girl with blonde locks in the middle of the group.

'That's Mabel,' said Teleri, her voice rising an octave. 'I never knew her well, for she was younger than me and so our paths rarely crossed as children. Elis, though, saw her as being like a younger sister.'

'He must have been devastated when she passed away,' I added. Teleri nodded plaintively. 'Her death brought misery to the whole house.'

The air went quiet for a few moments, when, suddenly, Holmes unceremoniously lifted the picture off its hook.

'Holmes, what the devil are you doing?!' I blasted.

'Teleri, with your permission, I need to look at this more closely,' Holmes said in the level tone of a police inspector, leaving the girl little choice but to say yes.

'Really, Holmes, this is beyond the pale,' I continued.

My companion ignored my protests and took the frame into the dining room, resting it on the table-top where there was most light. I sat with him, huffing my indignation but secretly hoping to be drawn into his confidence. Instead, he ignored me as he perused the photograph.

He briefly went upstairs to retrieve his magnifying glass from his bags but then continued to ignore me for another half an hour, until he suddenly announced he was to retire for the evening and informed me I was to rise at seven o'clock in the morning ready for the day's investigation.

I soon followed suit and announced to Teleri and to Kitty that I was going to bed. Together, we executed one final check of the locks and left for our chambers.

Elis's single bed where I was to sleep was hard and narrow, designed for a child. I imagined most of the rooms would be arranged in this way, with few changes made since the orphans left.

My face was pressed against the wall to my left, the wallpaper covered in illustrations of toy soldiers, faded over the years.

I drifted into a heavy sleep quicker than I expected. The surge of adrenaline that came in the showdown with that beast had subsided and the fatigue of a day's travel took hold. Barely two minutes passed after I dimmed my lamp before I felt my conscious thoughts morphing into surreal dreams and I was soon fast asleep.

I do not know how long I had been sleeping before I became conscious of a voice. Quiet and gentle at first, I presumed it was part of a dream.

'Dr Watson… Dr Watson…'

For the first few seconds of consciousness, I could not remember where I was, assuming I was back in Baker Street.

The room was pitch-black but my hand was pressed against textured wallpaper and I remembered the childlike pictures of soldiers.

'Dr Watson…'

The voice was a girl's. A young girl's. A long way away, but also crystal clear.

'Dr Watson…'

I thought of Mabel.

'Dr Watson…'

The child's sweet voice used the intonation of a prayer being recited, or a nursery rhyme sung in the schoolyard. 'Dr Watson…'

All sleep had left me now as I took in what I was hearing. Was Mabel calling my name as the next victim? I sat up in bed and pressed my head against the wall. It sounded like the voice was coming from within the wall itself.

I tried to gather my thoughts, and to think as logically as possible. My first instinct was to knock on the other adjoining room, to my right opposite the bed, where I knew Sherlock Holmes was sleeping. But I knew that any sound from me might alert the little girl and I was desperate to know the root of this ghostly call.

Carefully, I slid my body off the bed and placed my feet on the carpeted floor. I turned the gas up on my lamp to provide some light. I pulled myself to a standing position and took my first step away from my bed and towards the door.

'Dr Watson!' Mabel's voice was firmer now, as if shocked by something. 'Dr Watson!…' She was scared.

I resisted the urge to hurry my actions and continued to creep to the door. I turned the doorknob as slowly as possible, so the click was barely perceptible to the human ear.

I placed a bare foot onto the wooden floor of the landing. As I pressed my weight down, I realised the floorboard moved slightly and would likely creak should I place more pressure upon it. I reversed and then stepped onto a different, firmer board. In two light steps, I was at the door to the room where, it seemed, the voice emanated.

'Dr Watson, please…' came a tearful cry. I did not believe in spirits, but this voice – wherever it was from – was pleading for my help.

I softly placed my fingers on the handle into the next room, slowly gripping it until I was entirely confident that I could turn it and enter in one swift move.

In a single click, I entered the room, flashing my lantern into it.

All I saw was the outline of a figure – a girl – slumped in the corner on a rocking chair. She was limp and lifeless, but the rocking chair tipped gently back and forth.

I yelled out in shock and held the lamp up to cast more light across the room. But the figure in the chair was not a person – it was a large ragdoll, its grotesque face smiling mockingly at me. But what had made the chair rock?

'Dr Watson…' And then, another name: '…Teleri…'

I froze again. The voice was still there, no louder than when I was in my own bed, as if perpetually out of reach, but the direction changed when it said Teleri's name.

I approached the ragdoll and placed my hand on the arm of the chair to stop it rocking.

'Dr Watson?...'

The voice was behind me now! Closer, more real.

I swung round to see Teleri stood behind me in her nightdress. 'Sorry, I haven't been able to sleep – Mabel's voice... It was calling me. I saw the light on the landing and thought it was her.'

'What?!' I gasped. 'She was using my name as well. I thought it was coming from in here...'

'This is her old room, Dr Watson. I've been sleeping in the chamber to the other side of it. Whenever she calls out, it sounds like it's from in here, but there's nothing. I've checked every morning after it's happened.'

'And the rocking chair...' I said.

'Was it moving?' she asked. 'It always is when I've heard the voice and come in here.'

I nodded. 'Is it true that Elis heard that same voice?'

'Yes, Doctor. He never believed in such things and yet he was driven quite mad by it,' she replied. 'It's a portent of doom... It seems we're both being warned,' Teleri said, 'or perhaps we're being chosen?...'

V. The Keys to the Mystery

'I'm pleased, Watson, that you left the everything just as it was in the night.' Sherlock Holmes traced his finger along the edge of the carpet.

I had barely slept another wink after hearing Mabel's voice. Teleri and I returned to our rooms though I just lay on the bed, counting the soldiers on the wall, occasionally drifting in and out of slumber and eerie half-dreams. There had been no more cries from beyond the grave and so, at six o'clock, I had woken Holmes, billeted in the room next to mine. It was still dark though the first sounds of the lark could be heard over the hills outside. Against his initial protestations (for he had hoped to remain undisturbed until seven) I had reported my tale of the night before, piquing his interest.

'Watson, help me move your bed,' ordered Holmes. We shimmied the wrought-iron frame a couple of feet from the wall, allowing my friend to inspect the area more closely. He blew the dust from the edge of the carpet and crouched down, peering intently through his looking glass. He stopped suddenly; a moment of revelation.

He pinched some kind of yellow substance gathered on the floor between two fingers and placed it onto the top of a chest of drawers.

'What is it, Holmes?' I asked.

'Wax…'

'Many candles would have been lit in this room, and it does not look as if it's been cleaned in this spot for some time.'

'This is fresh wax.' Holmes placed a fragment on his tongue. 'And it's not the paraffin or stearin that one would most commonly find in candles.'

'And, Holmes, this bed has been moved recently,' I observed.

Holmes lifted himself up to stand beside me. 'We'll make a detective of you yet, Watson,' he smiled sardonically. The old indentations in the carpet left by the feet of the bed were pronounced and darker in colour, the dust barely gathered over the years. But an inch along from those dents were fresher patches where the bed had been placed back in the past few days. The carpet was squashed down, but thick dust still present.

'Watson, look in your medical bag. Do you have a thick scalpel? Anything with which I can jimmy this open.' Holmes fingered the edge of a small air vent nailed into the wall.

I passed him a blunt blade from the bottom of my bag. After a minute of prising and pulling, he forced the vent free of the wall, then looked inside the cavity between my room and Mabel's. On first sight, it was an empty shell, a foot deep. Holmes reached into it and tapped the vent opposite that would face out into Mabel's bedroom. In contrast to the vent he had just prised open, the other one rattled loosely in its socket.

When Holmes pulled his hand from the gap, he was holding another small mound of the strange wax in his palm; thin peelings of yellow.

Holmes and I then explored Mabel's old bedroom next door. The same findings were found – the bed moved then restored close to its original position – and wax gathered around the vent and just inside the wall. Similarly, the vent that would border Teleri's room had the same peelings of wax.

My companion was like a bloodhound now, his mind set only on the mystery. 'Watson, the rest of the house is rising. I still know little of the layout of this house. I should like you to go downstairs as normal but find out which room is directly beneath us. I do not want anyone alerted to our peculiar discovery just yet.'

I dressed hurriedly then descended past the framed photograph of the orphans, placed back on display. I could hear Garfield discussing the weather with the cook and Kitty in the dining room. I was pleased to hear he was in more cheerful spirits this morning.

The curtains each side of the hallway window were pulled open and one could immediately feel that the low sun was warmer than in previous days, promising a slight thaw.

I double-backed down a short corridor, attempting to locate the position directly beneath my and Mabel's rooms at the back of the house. Satisfied I was close to the correct position, I went to open an internal door. It was locked and with no key.

I returned upstairs and reported this to Holmes. On my friend's orders, I then joined Garfield at the breakfast table. The host's pleasure in my company was rather endearing, and he merrily quizzed me on some of my past adventures with Sherlock Holmes. Naturally, he was keen to discuss the report that my editor had labelled *The Hound of the Baskervilles* about his distant cousins' battle with a supposedly spectral dog. It was clear he knew the story off by heart, but he seemed thrilled to hear me narrate the ending of that particular tale when Holmes and I discovered that beast from Hell to be none other than a larger mongrel coated in phosphorus, unleashed on the moors to strike fear into Sir Henry Baskerville, the heir to the estate.

'I have never met that family line,' Garfield smiled. 'And I must admit I was glad to be some distance from it when these adventures became apparent. I should like to meet Sir Henry one day, though.'

'He is a decent fellow,' I recalled. 'I hear he is happily wed now, and that despicable curse has been put to rest.'

'But I fear it has come to Baskerville Court, Doctor.' Garfield's eyes blazed with fear. 'That monster last night... It was not of this world, of that I'm sure.'

'One thing I have found through my many years in the company of Sherlock Holmes, is that there is always a logical explanation,' I tried to reassure him. 'We shall find out what it is and then put a stop to whatever plagues this house...'

A different voice joined the conversation from behind my back. 'So, I assume the voice of little Mabel can be added to that list of rational phenomena, Dr Watson?' It was Teleri, freshly risen from bed, but looking as tired as I felt.

'You heard her again, Teleri?' Garfield asked desperately. 'She called out to you?'

Teleri nodded. 'And also to Dr Watson.'

'Doctor, why didn't you say?' Garfield begged.

'I didn't want to alarm you,' I replied. 'And I am sure there will be a most mundane explanation.'

Kitty served boiled eggs and buttered toast and I let the conversation progress before asking about the locked room. 'I wondered what the rooms in the house are used for,' I said innocently, 'in order to assist us in better securing the property. I notice the back room is locked.'

Garfield balked for a second.

'You must mean the music room, Dr Watson,' Teleri ventured. 'I've still never seen inside. Apparently, Garfield loved to play the piano and also the violin. He used to teach some of the children also.'

He blushed a little. 'Teleri is correct that I used to play,' he explained, 'but once the happiness left this house, so did the music. Mabel, you see, was especially musical. We spent many hours in that room, making music – she had a most prodigious ear. When she became ill, she was quarantined in that room in order to preserve her from scaling the stairs. I've never used the room since and prefer to keep it closed.'

'Elis talked about the joy the children would gain from the instruments in that room,' Teleri smiled. 'And he spoke of a gramophone – the first anyone had seen in this area! Elis was fascinated with it! I would love to look inside, if I may? Do you still have your violin, Garfield? A Stradivarius, wasn't it?'

'Stradivarius?!' a cheerful voice boomed. It was Holmes. He flashed me a surreptitious glance which told me he had the solution to the mystery just an arm's length away. 'You must know, Garfield, that I am something of an enthusiastic amateur on the instrument, though I profess to more than a little expertise. I should very much like to play a Stradivarius.'

Garfield's face flooded a bright puce. His reluctance to open the room was evident, though suddenly he had three pairs of eyes staring pleadingly, including his detective hero keen to try out his priceless violin.

Garfield reached inside his shirt to reveal a thin chain around his neck. Attached to the chain were two keys: a larger, heavy key, slightly rusted, so presumably for an outside door, and a smaller, polished indoor key. It was the indoor one he gripped in is fingers as he led us towards the sealed music room door.

He leaned forward to allow the chain enough slack to reach the lock, when we were all startled by a sudden bloodcurdling scream!

As one, we ran back into the dining room. Kitty was frozen in terror, staring outside at the garden.

'What is it, dear Kitty?' asked Teleri.

'The dog...' she whispered. 'The dog was back...Out there.' She pointed at the snow-covered lawn.

Holmes was first out the front door. I was surprised to see he already had his revolver on his person. He scanned the horizon and then looked down at the snow for footprints, like a tracker native to the Americas. He carefully skirted the lawn up to a low hedge and then followed it around the house.

'What can you see, Holmes?' I asked, deliberately staying some steps behind for fear of disturbing the scene.

'Not a thing...' Methodically, he shortened the circle he was tracing, walking slowly back and forth. 'The only prints are outside the hedge, and they're frozen, so they're from last night.' He indicated the massive pawprints. It was striking what a beast this thing was, its feet as wide as a cougar's.

Holmes approached a small dark circle of mud, uncovered by snow. It was the place where Garfield had been digging frantically the previous evening.

Holmes turned to the front door, where Teleri and Garfield waited, the latter cowering in the lady's arms. The poor man was terrified of the prospect of the beast's return.

'Get back inside!' ordered Holmes. 'And lock the door!'

I joined my friend's side. 'Don't fear, Watson,' he said to me, 'as no beast is in our midst at present... Not since last night. But I need some time here without them.'

'Then what did the maid see?' I enquired.

'A figment of her imagination, perhaps...' he pondered. 'Now it is light and new snow no longer falls, I want to inspect the grounds before we go to the village. I suggest you get your pistol first, Watson, just in case that animal should pay us a visit, and then check all the external doors. Did you see Garfield's key – not for the music room, but that old one he also had on the chain?'

'Like a dungeon keeper's?'

'Yes,' smiled Holmes. 'I'm presuming Baskerville Court doesn't have a dungeon, so let's find what he uses it for. It's clearly important to him if he keeps it on his person at all times.'

I went inside to retrieve my weapon and our coats, informing the others to remain indoors.

Holmes and I went our separate ways, checking each external door and window. None of the locks were big enough to require such a key as the one Garfield kept on his person. We fanned out from the house to broaden our search, though Holmes focused on the front of the property, close to where Garfield was digging the previous night, and the same spot Teleri said she found him on the night of Elis's death.

I searched the stables, though no key was required on the bolted gate, and then a small gardening shed. All around I looked, scouring the land until, when I turned around, the house was perhaps a quarter of a mile away. Mercifully, the air was warmer than it had been, and I even unbuttoned my greatcoat amid the exertion of the hunt. There seemed to be no sign of another outhouse or building of any sort. I was about to end my search when I trudged onto a hard surface. I pressed down with my boot and felt a bang, rather than the scrunch of snow and grass elsewhere. Curious, I began to claw at the snow and ice to see what lay beneath. Quickly, a wooden hatch was revealed under the whiteness, around five feet by five. I took it to be an underground wood cellar, where chopped logs would be stored for winter.

I leaned closer and found the lock. It was large and rusted. Although I had no access to the key – it would still be with Garfield – I was certain this must be the lock that corresponded to it.

I ran back to Holmes who was already rounding the corner. I pointed out my discovery.

'Excellent, Watson!' Holmes applauded. 'I have also made a discovery of my own,' he revealed, pulling out a strange pencil-sized tube of ivory and metal. At one end was what appeared to be a mouthpiece like a cornet's, but at the other was a small bulbous pump. It looked like a surgical device, but none that I recognised.

'What is it?' I asked.

'I'm not yet sure,' said Holmes, 'but we will soon find out… Now, we shall not mention this to the household. Let us go to the village as we need to inspect Elis's body. But when we return here later, it is imperative we somehow get hold of those keys. I have a feeling they will lead us to the answers we seek.'

VI. The Next Victim

Teleri took us to the quiet village of Meifod in the same two-horse carriage we had used the day before. It was a relief to see the snow beginning to melt on lower ground, though the hills around us were still a majestic sweep of white. 'We've been covered in snow for over a fortnight,' said Teleri. 'It shall be a relief to see the green reappear on the hills.'

Teleri led us to the undertaker's. She became quiet as we entered the village, though this was to be expected as we approached the black-fronted building where Elis still lay. Elis's funeral had been delayed over the Christmas period and so his corpse was being preserved in readiness for his burial in a few days. Understandably, she felt no urge to once again see the body of her sweetheart and, besides, she had received a message that a letter awaited her at the post office. She hoped it would be a missive from her dear sister Catrin in London. She left us at the door and arranged to return in an hour.

We entered the establishment, removing our hats out of respect for our surroundings. There was nobody inside the parlour, dimly lit only by a small shaft of light cast in from a high window. Two coffins were laid out, open, though I was relieved they were not yet occupied.

The air was thick with the grim silence of death, broken only by the sound of someone moving in the back room.

Tentatively, I cleared my throat in order to attract the proprietor's attention. Slow footsteps came our way. An elderly gentleman dressed in black tails and tie, his face as white as his hair, sombrely entered the room.

I introduced myself, involuntarily whispering, though it seemed appropriate. 'Sir, my name is Dr Watson, and this is my companion, Mr-...'

'Sherlock Holmes!' the old man roared, not unlike Garfield's greeting the evening prior. It seemed Holmes was revered in this part of the country. All funereal convention disappeared as this gaunt old man realised he was face to face with someone so famous. 'How marvellous!... And you, Dr Watson, you're older in real life! I heard you were visiting the area.'

I scoffed my objections, though the undertaker's good spirits were infectious. He shook our hands. 'Mordecai Roberts, servant to the living – and the dead!'

I was struck dumb by the man's good humour. Holmes reciprocated the handshake. 'It is indeed a pleasure, Mordecai, to meet a former man of Llandovery College!'

Mordecai looked quizzically at Holmes.

'The motto carved into the hearth,' my friend continued. *'Gwell Dysg na Golud...* Excuse my poor Welsh pronunciation but that is the motto of that esteemed school, is it not?...'

'Education is preferable to wealth,' Mordecai roared his approval. My friend was performing the part of the great Sherlock Holmes of my stories in order to ingratiate us with our host, and it worked superbly.

'Ha, Watson!' Mordecai cried giddily. 'He really is as you write him, sir! *Duw, Duw*... what an honour.'

In moments, Mordecai was leading us through to a stable across the backyard. 'I'm the only man in Meifod grateful for this arctic weather, gentlemen. It's meant poor young Elis has at least remained well preserved. Well, what's left of him.' I found his cheery off-handedness slightly distasteful.

He led us to a large plinth, a hessian blanket draped across the top. Mordecai whipped it off like it was part of a magician's act, revealing the mauled corpse of Elis Williams. His body was warped and twisted with large cavities where his stomach and throat should have been. The flesh and sinew inside his body had frozen solid. He reminded me of one of the preserved human specimens we would chop up in order to teach squeamish trainee medics at St Bart's the inner workings of the human body.

'The size of the jaws would indeed be consistent with the beast we saw last night, Watson...' Holmes whispered, leaning in to examine the body more closely.

'It appears his jugular was cut by the animal's incisors,' I surmised. 'Mercifully so, I would say, for the bruises around his trunk indicate a brutal struggle preceding his death.'

I looked closely at his left hand and noticed the upper part of the little finger was missing. I recalled Teleri telling us that was how she had initially identified him when she found him on the hills on Christmas morning.

'Is there any way of knowing how he gained that injury?' Holmes nodded to the finger I was examining.

'Not really.' I replied. 'It's undoubtedly an old wound – from childhood, as Teleri told us – and a clean break at the joint of the digit. I've seen many a butcher's boy with the same injury, chopped off in a single clean action. I've also treated poor wretches who have had their hands trapped in machinery and their fingers rarely heal as smoothly as Elis here.' I sensed the irony of us discussing an ancient injury when the rest of him lay savaged and battered, thrown around as if it were a ragdoll – an image that put in my mind the doll on the rocking chair in Mabel's bedroom.

Holmes turned to Mordecai. 'Mordecai, my good man, do you keep records of previous bodies you have prepared here?'

Mordecai looked at him uncertainly, though barely hiding his excitement at the prospect of assisting his hero. 'Of course, Mr Holmes.'

'How far do these records go back?' Holmes proceeded.

'Since the day I took over from my father, almost four decades now!' Mordecai reported proudly.

'So, Mabel Saunders would have come through here when she passed, I presume?' asked Holmes.

'Mabel-…? Oh, the little orphan at the Court? A couple of years ago, she went, didn't she?' asked Mordecai, to which Holmes nodded. The undertaker continued: 'I'm sorry, Mr Holmes, but I know she didn't come to me, poor thing. You know, I always remember the children – the adults, well, that's part of life, the natural order of things – but, even for an undertaker, a child's body is a horrible business, and something one never becomes used to… I remember all the children I've buried, but Mabel went elsewhere.'

'Why would that be? You're the only undertaker for some miles?' Holmes pressed.

'I recall poor old Garfield made other plans for her,' he replied, scratching the white hairs on his head. 'I assumed she perhaps had family wherever she came from, so perhaps they dealt with the funeral.'

It seemed unlikely, as any other family would presumably have taken an orphan in while she was still living. Both Holmes and I paused to consider this.

'Terrible business, gents, terrible business…' Mordecai shook his head, before tactlessly changing tack. 'Still, you will join me for a *paned-* sorry, a cup of tea. Oh, and I've brought in some *bara brith* that Mrs Roberts had left over from Christmas.'

'Mordecai!' A man's shout bellowed out from inside the parlour. The undertaker hurried inside, leaving Holmes and I to peruse Elis's corpse a few moments longer.

After a minute, Mordecai returned. 'Alas, the *bara brith* will have to wait,' he reported. 'I have a new body to tend to.'

Two burly farmhands followed Mordecai across the yard and into the stable. They carried the lifeless body of a man dressed all in black and rested it on the plinth beside Elis. Chunks of his body were missing, his abdomen and upper thighs.

'Haydn Lewis…' mumbled one of the carriers.

'Where did you find him?' asked Holmes.

'A mile from Baskerville Court,' he replied. 'Poor Haydn never came home after searching for Caradog's dogs. We found him this morning near our flock. Torn to shreds, he was, as well as half of our ewes. It's one big animal that's out there.'

'Like *Cŵn Annwn* had got hold of them all…' lamented the other yokel.

'Cŵn…?'

'Cŵn Annwn,' repeated Mordecai. 'A Welsh legend. They're a pack of hounds sent from the underworld to claim any wrongdoers. Except Haydn was no wrongdoer…'

'Most decent man you could meet,' said the first farmhand. 'How he could work for that bastard, Caradog, I'll never know.

'Cŵn Annwn… a myth not unlike the Hound of the Baskervilles in Devon…' I thought aloud.

We were about to leave Mordecai to his work when Holmes swivelled on his heels to address the farm workers who had brought him in.

'Are you shepherds familiar with this instrument?' Holmes pulled from his coat pocket the strange device he had found in the front of Baskerville Court, the cylinder of ivory and metal…

We waited for Teleri beside the carriage, the horses tethered to a post on the village high street, just a few yards from Mordecai Roberts's. She was still inside the post office and we were both content to stand in the pleasant sunshine, the first whiff of spring threatening the snow.

'I have a feeling there may be two mysteries at play here, Watson…' said Holmes as he took the first drag of tobacco from a freshly-lit pipe. 'But we need to get into that wood cellar for me to be certain. Until then, we keep our counsel.'

Teleri reappeared, clutching a formal-looking letter in a brown envelope, the name and address carefully typed.

'I'm sorry I kept you, gentlemen,' she apologised. 'The postmaster needed me to sign some forms before releasing this letter.'

'Is it from your sister?' I asked.

'It's from a solicitor,' she said, a trace of confusion in her voice, 'with the express order that it must only be opened *after* Elis's funeral.'

'His last will and testament, perhaps?' I pondered.

'I very much doubt he had any worldly goods to pass on,' she said, staring at the unopened envelope as if somehow its contents might magically present themselves to her through the paper.

I had the grave duty of reporting Haydn's demise. The poor woman was deeply saddened, describing him in the same glowing terms as Mordecai and the shepherds.

'You will stop this beast, won't you, sirs?' she pleaded. 'I beg you.'

When we returned to Baskerville Court, Garfield Baskerville-Wilkes was pacing back and forth in front of the house. As we neared, we could hear him rhythmically muttering the same refrain. 'This just won't do… This just won't do…'

'Garfield, you must go inside,' said Teleri warmly from her driver's platform. 'You're not even wearing a coat.'

Garfield regarded us as if he had not heard the carriage approach, let alone pull up beside him. His joy at our arrival was warm and genuine. 'Teleri, my dear! Ah, and our revered guests…' he shook our hands as we descended the step from the carriage. 'A pleasant morning, I trust. I think the cook has prepared lunch though I have business to attend to here. You carry on without me…'

He was scanning the ground, presumably looking for the very object the shepherds in Meifod had just identified, still concealed in Holmes's pocket.

Teleri disappeared to her room after we had taken luncheon. I presumed she may secretly open her letter from the solicitor, for anyone would be deeply tempted given the same situation. 'Not to be opened until after Elis's funeral,' she had recited aloud, as if talking herself out of succumbing to temptation. However, perhaps its contents would be too much to resist and, in truth, I could see little harm in her opening it before her fiancé's burial two days hence.

Holmes observed Garfield from the drawing room window. Thinner patches of snow around the house were melting in the afternoon sunshine, though it was still cold. Occasionally, Garfield would drag his hand through a shallow puddle or turn over a chunk of ice, all to no avail in his search. At least he now wore a coat – taken out to him by Kitty at

Teleri's insistence – and, though clearly in a state of confusion, he appeared to be of no danger to himself.

Though we could hear nothing from inside the house, we noticed Garfield became alerted by something in the distance. Both Holmes and I instinctively reached inside our suit pockets, our revolvers poised just in case of such a moment. Was this another invasion by the hound?

We pressed our faces up to the glass and saw what had disturbed Garfield. Lord Caradog on his stallion, a look of indignant anger upon his face.

Presently, we strode outside.

'I hold you responsible for my stableman's death, Baskerville,' Caradog hollered at Garfield. 'He was found near your land, savaged by an animal that – I can assure you – is not from my estate.'

'Greetings, Lord Caradog,' Garfield smiled, maintaining a veneer of pleasantness. 'I was so sorry to hear about Haydn. A good fellow he was.'

'I didn't care much for the man, but he had a deftness with the animals which will not be so easy to replace,' whined the lord, pulling his horse to a shaky stop in front of Garfield.

'I don't know how I can help you though, Caradog,' Garfield protested. 'Although I regret that I may have inadvertently attracted this scourge into our midst – it seems my whole family is cursed.'

'So, you accept your responsibility for this business,' quipped Caradog. I could sense he was seeking to take advantage of Garfield's weak mental state.

'I'm sorry, Lord Caradog, but Mr Baskerville-Wilkes bears no responsibility for this,' I cut in. Caradog looked disappointed to see me and Holmes emerge from the house. 'I ask that you leave him in peace.'

'My family once owned all this land – everything you can see, from the English border up to the River Vyrnwy,' Caradog boasted. 'We defended protectors of the Crown throughout the English Civil War – friends of the King who fled battle in England in order to seek refuge. It was the Caradogs who saved them and assured their safety until the conclusion of that war.'

I recalled Caradog boasting of this when he confronted Teleri on our arrival to the area. The aristocrat continued with scarcely a breath. 'The parish was all the better for it: one family presiding over all local matters. Without the Caradogs, those loyal servants to the King would have perished and the history of this isle may well have been very different… But since my father sold this part of our land in a moment of weakness to Wilfred Baskerville-Wilkes, all that history has been destroyed.'

'So, where did your family sequester these refugees of the English Civil War?' It was Holmes. I felt his question to be irrelevant in the context of our situation and feared it would only fan Caradog's inflated ego.

The lord's puffed-out demeanour relaxed slightly at Holmes's strange question. I imagined he had regaled many an unsuspecting underling with his ancestors' story and perhaps this might be the first time anyone had displayed any hint of interest.

'Tunnels, sir,' he chirruped. 'A network of underground tunnels kept the escapees out of sight of those blasted Roundheads.'

'And where are those tunnels now?' asked Holmes innocently.

'I-... I don't know,' Caradog admitted with a hint of diffidence. If nothing else, Holmes's strategy had taken some of the wind from the brute's sails.

Garfield looked as confused as me at his line of questioning.

'Tunnels... Most interesting,' my companion concluded with a hint of sarcasm. 'I should very much like to discuss this historical period further, but I fear our stay here is but a short one.'

'You would be most welcome at my house, Mr Holmes,' Caradog offered. 'It is a pleasure to meet a man who appreciates my family's deeds.'

'Alas, we should be gone in the morning, sir,' replied Holmes, the confidence in this statement surprising both Garfield and me. 'Next time, perhaps.'

Soothed by Holmes's good spirit, Caradog pulled on his horse's reins and steered away.

'Contemptible man...' Garfield muttered.

'I couldn't agree more,' nodded Holmes.

Sherlock Holmes had rarely been so complimented to the point of being deified as he had been these past twenty-four hours. I was beginning to itch to return to the more anonymous metropolis of London.

'You say we'll be gone tomorrow, Holmes?' I mentioned as we returned into the warm, Garfield remaining outside.

Holmes flashed me a knowing smile. 'I would wager this mystery – or, indeed, mysteries – will be solved by then…'

VII. A Night of Discoveries

Night fell early in the valley, the sun hidden by the hills before four o'clock. Teleri assured us she had not opened the mysterious letter, regarding it as a final promise to Elis. The instruction explicitly stated that the contents were not to be revealed until after his funeral, so she assumed it to be a last wish of his and so disrespectful to dishonour it.

Garfield finally returned indoors. He seemed more troubled after his day's fruitless searching. The darkness brought with it a state of melancholy in him, terror just beneath the surface. He continued to pace the house but this time inside, staring out of the windows, awaiting his fate.

As it grew late, Holmes rightly suggested I offer him a sedative as I had the previous night. Thankfully, there were no beastly howls from outside tonight, but Garfield continued to be in a state of agitation.

Garfield accepted a sedative but only if we promised him we would keep watch. He asked Kitty to check all the doors and windows again, downstairs and up. She did so (in spite of carrying out the same task only an hour earlier) before Garfield accepted my gentle narcotic which came in the form of a large pill.

Teleri ascended the stairs shortly afterwards before Holmes and I took our leave, leaving Kitty and the cook preparing the kitchen for breakfast.

Sleep took some time to come that night. I kept my lamp partially lit, again staring at the soldiers on Elis's bedroom wall. Naturally, I was all too conscious that Mabel's ghostly voice may come at any moment and, like a frightened child, I barely dared close my eyes. I was certain there must be a rational explanation, but I could not find it, however hard I thought.

I had not been in my chambers for more than five minutes when the voice came once again…

'Dr Watson…' Mabel's sing-song voice. Innocent yet sinister, all at once.

'Dr Watson…'

The second call convinced me I was not dreaming. I repeated my actions of the previous night, carefully swinging my legs out of the bed and onto the soft carpet. Except, this time, I grabbed my gun which lay on the bedside table.

'Dr Watson… Dr Watson…' Just like the previous evening, her voice started to become frightened, more desperate. 'Dr Watson…'

I edged out onto the landing, avoiding the same wooden floorboard I recalled from before. Slowly, I reached for the door handle with my left hand, my pistol firmly in my right, finger hovering beside the trigger.

Click… The doorknob turned more firmly than I wanted. It was only a split-second, but I knew I had to act instantly if I were to retain the advantage of surprise.

I burst in to Mabel's bedroom. A tall figure awaited me on the inside of the door, instinctively grabbing my right wrist to deflect the gun away from him.

'Watson, dear boy! You're going to like this…' It was Sherlock Holmes.

Hurriedly, he showed me in, closing the door behind us. There, again, was the doll on the rocking chair. 'This is ingenious, Watson…' Holmes said as he squatted besides the chair. He held something up in his hand, but I couldn't see what. 'Look closer,' he urged.

Between his fingers was an almost imperceptible length of wire, no thicker than a piece of horse hair. It extended from the bottom of the skirting board at one side of the room all the way to the other. On its journey, it was threaded around the struts at the base of the rocking chair.

Holmes took one end of the wire and began to slowly pull it. As he did so, the chair began to tip backwards and forwards and I could see the string winding its way into the wall, and through the vent Holmes had inspected that morning.

As it was winding, the first strain of a girl's voice could be heard: 'Dr Watson… Dr Watson…' It was Mabel!

'Good grief, Holmes!' I spat. 'How on Earth does this work?'

Holmes slid off the vent, loose on this side of the wall. 'Look inside…'

I peered into the cavity between Mabel's room and mine. The wire was connected to a small metallic machine wedged inside the gap. I recognised it instantly, although this was clearly a dated prototype model. It was a gramophone or, more accurately, one of the first phonographs! Atop the phonograph was a yellow-brown reel. As Holmes pulled the wire, it slowly turned the reel. A small stylus, two inches in length, scraped into the reel, producing the sound of the little girl's voice, which came out of a small amplifying horn.

'So, this explains the wax you found here this morning, Holmes!' I blurted, seeing how the wax fell away as the stylus cut into it. 'But how did this machine get here? It wasn't here when we checked earlier.'

'Whoever's doing this has clearly been very careful to cover their tracks each day,' said Holmes. He then led me to the string at the other side of the room. Inside the chasm between Mabel's room and where Teleri was sleeping, was another small phonograph machine. When Holmes pulled the string, it played Mabel's voice again, only this time she called for Teleri.

'But how was this operated last night, Holmes?' I demanded. 'There was no-one in this room!'

'See the back of the chair,' indicated Holmes. 'There are two pieces of wire, each operating its own phonograph. They are wound tightly around the feet of the rocking chair and then angled towards the edge of the carpet. I believe some of these floors and spaces between walls have been excavated in order to accommodate the wire and the sound machines.'

'Hence the cold wind that blasts through the house upstairs!' I exclaimed. 'And where do the wires lead?... Surely, they will lead us to the hoaxer who's frightening us with this ghostly trick.'

'Precisely, Watson... They go straight down from this chamber and into the room below...'

'The music room!' I remembered.

At that moment, the wires began to stretch taut again, but this time it was not Holmes moving them.

'Dr Watson... Teleri...' The ghostly voice echoed from each wall.

'But Garfield has the key to the music room,' I said. 'And that sedative I gave him would have knocked him out for a good few hours.'

'There is one other person who would have access to the music room,' said Holmes in a level tone. 'Watson... Follow me.'

Stealthily, we descended the stairs. Holmes pondered the old group photograph a moment as we passed, a half-smile on his lips.

We headed towards the back of Baskerville Court along the short rear corridor. The music room door was shut fast, but we could clearly hear movement inside. The slight squeak of a handle being turned inside.

To my surprise, rather than await the culprit to come out of the room, Holmes took a more direct line of action. He knocked on the door!

'Kitty, please allow us in,' he announced calmly. 'I can assure you we mean you no harm.'

I confess to being at a disadvantage, eagerly trying to follow Holmes's train of thought. *Kitty the maid?!*

A moment passed before the lock clicked and the door knob turned open. Kitty stood inside the door, her head hung in shame. For all her sixteen years, at this moment she looked more like a chided schoolgirl in the headmaster's office.

'Mr Holmes, Dr Watson... I'm so sorry,' she spluttered, before bursting into tears and falling into my arms.

VIII. A Confession

Knowing the game was up, Kitty mournfully showed us into the music room and shut the door. It was a large chamber though the furniture, as well as what I took to be a piano and a cello, was covered in dustsheets.

The long wires we had found upstairs in Mabel's old room were pulled taut through a gap in the coving at the edge of the ceiling above. At the bottom of the wires, Kitty had wound them tightly around a turning handle improvised from a Singer sewing machine. A simple yet ingenious contraption.

'Ah, I thought so!' roared Holmes triumphantly. 'It was the yellow wax that told me, Watson, that a phonograph had been used – the needle scraping into the reel makes the vibrations that cause sound!'

'Why would you commit such a tasteless prank, Kitty?' I began. 'Why would you try to terrify both me and Teleri out of our wits?'

Kitty searched for an explanation, but nothing came.

'And poor Elis!' I continued. 'He lost his mind at the sound of that voice! It led to his death!'

Again, Kitty sobbed. Despite the gravity of her misdemeanour, I felt sorry for the girl, and I noticed Holmes used a soothing tone which betrayed some sentiment towards the maid.

'Is it your voice on the recording?' he asked.

She nodded, looking more and more pale. 'I would place the phonograph machines in the gaps in the walls each night when I checked the locks in the house,' she said, 'and then retrieve them when I lit the fires before dawn each morning. I would play them by turning this handle.'

'Why would you do this?' I spluttered.

'You wanted revenge for the death of little Mabel Saunders,' Holmes said. 'You were related, were you not?'

Kitty collapsed to the floor.

Five minutes passed before Kitty was revived with the help of some smelling salts that I had retrieved from my medical bag upstairs.

The maid slowly composed herself. 'Mabel was my cousin.'

'I recognised the likeness in that photograph of the orphans,' said Holmes.

'She would write to my mother and me,' Kitty elaborated. 'We would have cared for her ourselves, but we were in service in a house in Wolverhampton and so we were unable to give her a home. But she was happy enough here, she said... Happy until a year before she died.'

Kitty began to cry again, barely able to contemplate what had led to this night.

'We just wanted to scare him...' was all Kitty could offer.

'Scare who?' I demanded, before answering my own question. 'To scare Elis?... But why?' I asked.

'No, not Elis! It wasn't Elis I wanted to frighten...' she sniffed.

I failed to follow her line of thought.

'You wanted to frighten Garfield…' Holmes cut in. It was a statement more than a question.

Silence filled the room.

'What? What in God's name is going on?' I asked, aiming the question at both Holmes and the maid.

Kitty took a long sip from a glass of water. She was ready to reveal the truth.

'It was Elis and me,' she explained. 'We both wanted to frighten Garfield.'

'But you scared Elis to such an extent, he fled the house and into the snow!' I bellowed.

'No, no,' she sobbed. 'Elis and I planned it all together! We wanted Garfield and also the cook to hear Elis's name being called by Mabel so we formulated this plan to use the phonographs and for me to record a voice that might sound like my cousin's.

'You see, before poor Auntie Lynwen died, she had been driven insane by voices in her head… She said she could hear Mabel calling to her in the night. Of course, we knew it was her mind, wrought mad by the loss of one of her beloved orphans, but after Lynwen died, Garfield became terrified of Mabel calling to him. He was already of a vulnerable disposition. But he became more and more paranoid…'

Holmes elucidated: 'Mabel had known something about Garfield… when she was still alive… A secret. A secret Garfield desperately wanted to remain undiscovered.'

Kitty whimpered a yes.

'And am I right in thinking Elis knew that secret of Garfield's too?' Holmes pressed. Again, the girl nodded.

'H-... How do you know this, Holmes?' I stammered.

'The missing finger,' he replied. 'Elis's missing finger.'

'How can Elis's missing finger tell you all that?' I demanded.

'His wound was old, from infancy, and yet his sweetheart Teleri did not know how he received it. That, in itself, is strange, don't you think?... Invariably, there's a famous tale behind any childhood injury, a story re-told often by the bearer. But not in this case.'

I followed Holmes's line of reasoning though it did not explain the whole story. He took a moment to collect his thoughts before continuing: 'And then, when I looked at that photograph on the stairway, not only did Mabel resemble Kitty here, but I could make out – with the aid of my magnifying glass – that she also had part of her little finger missing on her left hand.'

'So, you presumed a connection?' I muttered.

'Two children from the same household, both with exactly the same injury... It would lead one to assume they had both been wounded in the same manner. Punished, perhaps, by the same master... I presumed by Garfield but I could not be completely certain.'

'You're right, Mr Holmes,' said Kitty. 'Garfield would punish anyone in the same way... Anyone who might expose who he really was... He would chop off a little finger as a warning to any child who might tell...'

Kitty cleared her throat. 'Auntie Lynwen had discovered that secret too. Not straight after Mabel's death, but a year later. It's what made her lose her mind – she had been perfectly fine before then... yes, she grieved for Mabel and lamented the closure of Baskerville Court to the orphans, but something – a discovery – made her snap. She began to hear Mabel's voice and, within a week, she was dead.'

'And, so, you wanted to emulate the same macabre call from the dead – in order to frighten Garfield?' asked Holmes.

'No-one knew I was Mabel's cousin – I gained employment here without mentioning that fact,' Kitty expanded. 'But I soon confided in Elis – I knew his missing finger meant he had suffered the same fate as Mabel and so I was confident he could be trusted.

'Mabel had written to me before she died, telling me of how Garfield had begun to torment her... to make her life a living Hell... And how Garfield Baskerville-Wilkes was not the fine upstanding gentleman everyone assumed him to be.'

My blood chilled at what this man must have done to little Mabel.

'Elis quickly confirmed this when I told him what Mabel had written to me,' Kitty reported sadly. 'The pair of us resolved to get our revenge on Garfield – for what he did to Mabel... and for what he did to Elis when he was a boy.'

'What did he do?' I asked, fearing the response.

Kitty could not find the words and so Holmes stepped in: 'I assume, Kitty, that Mabel and Elis had been victims of something unspeakable...'

It was rare I saw Holmes shocked by the depth of human wickedness, but his voice cracked a moment as he delivered the words: 'I take it Garfield Baskerville-Wilkes had a depraved predilection for the young... And he cut their fingers off as a warning never to tell of their master's horrific crimes against them. Am I right?'

Kitty looked us both in the eye, bravely holding back tears of anger. 'We thought we could make him go quite mad – to the point he would be committed to an asylum. I know it is not a godly thing that we did, but when you think of the awful crimes he committed on innocent children, it seemed an almost merciful punishment...

'Elis decided he would pretend to lose his mind after hearing Mabel call his name on Christmas Eve. We recorded my voice speaking to him. Elis then planned to run to Teleri's house – though she knew nothing of our plans, even to this day – and hide there until Garfield thought Mabel had claimed another victim, the same fate he believed had befallen Auntie Lynwen. We were then going to record my voice calling out for Garfield – we knew it would break him.

'And then, after Garfield was taken to the asylum, Elis would reappear alive and well...' The poor girl began to weep at the thought of Elis's actual fate. 'That was the plan...'

'But this doesn't explain why you then recorded my name on the phonograph machine, and Teleri's,' I said.

'I'm sorry, Dr Watson,' she confessed. 'I wanted you and Mr Holmes, and Teleri before, out the house... I wanted to finish Garfield alone, but I couldn't do it with you here. I needed good people out of the way, so I could finish what Elis and I started. For Elis… and for Mabel.'

There was one major thing that had been ignored up to this point, I thought…

'So how does this explain the dog that killed Elis?' I asked.

'I don't know…' cried Kitty. 'That beast had never been heard of until that night… Elis ran out into the hills as planned – we were never to know that such an animal was loose at the time.'

'That, Watson, is why I believe we have not one, but two mysteries,' announced Holmes. 'The mystery of Mabel's voice, and then the mystery of that hound… The mystery of the voice is one I am eager to overlook for the time being.'

Kitty's eyes flashed their gratitude momentarily. It was a fleeting moment of humanity from my companion, not unknown but decidedly rare.

'But the mystery of that hound is one that troubles me greatly…' Holmes continued. 'And I fear that that too leads to Garfield Baskerville-Wilkes…'

IX. The Tunnels

Holmes ordered Kitty to remain downstairs while he and I strode up towards Garfield's quarters to confront him. I was confident the nefarious individual would be deep in his slumbers following the sedative I had administered a few hours previously.

Holmes led the charge, pistol cocked. We pushed a thick oak door open and burst into his room. We rushed to his bed, poised to wake him and to demand answers. Holmes pulled the covers back. But his bed was empty!

'How could he?!' I blasted frustratedly.

Holmes stepped to his bedside table where he showed me a glass of water – and the pill I had given him earlier, unconsumed.

'The devious brute!' I roared.

Holmes dashed to the window, it was pulled wide open. I joined him and saw the sloping low roof that backed onto his room, providing an easy escape route towards the back garden.

In the distance, at the furthest end of the land that rolled northward, we both saw the yellow flicker of a lantern in the darkness.

'Garfield!' we exclaimed in unison.

In a flash, we descended the stairs. When Kitty saw us, she read our intentions and so scooped up our outdoor boots and presented us with our coats.

Snow was falling fast once again, the night temperature dropping like a stone. White flakes whipped into our faces as we sprinted into the icy wind.

We rounded the perimeter of the building until we were racing towards the faint light a quarter of a mile away. I could not work out if it was the howl of the wind or my imagination, but, for a moment, I swear I heard the baying of that deadly hound. I continued to run towards Garfield in the distance, ignoring any thought of that creature, for fear that any circumspection would only extinguish my courage.

Holmes stretched ahead, his rangy limbs propelling him forward. I struggled to keep up, though adrenaline aided me, coursing through my veins.

Soon, Garfield was illuminated by his lantern. He was unlocking the horizontal door in the earth. The door into the wood cellar.

He struggled with the oversized key he had kept around his neck, the old lock failing to comply as he turned the key.

We heard the click as the door finally agreed to open, and Holmes bounded forward. In one leap, my friend swooped at Garfield, grabbing at him before he could dip into the cellar. Holmes and Garfield tumbled into the hard, frozen turf next to the hole in the ground.

'You should let that hound come for me, Mr Holmes!' Garfield cried maniacally. 'This will all end soon – either with my death, or yours!'

Holmes and Garfield's bodies writhed together on the hard ground. Holmes's deceptive athleticism soon proved too much for his adversary, with my friend twisting the villain's forearm hard behind his back. Garfield yelped in pain.

'We know what you did, Baskerville!' announced Holmes confidently. 'You brought evil to this house. A place your father wanted to be a refuge for orphans has been sullied by your despicable acts.'

'You sound like Lynwen! That old woman was driven mad when she discovered this place… She went so mad she threw herself to her own death!' Garfield cried triumphantly.

Holmes and I took in what he had said. The matron to the orphans must have finally found out his secret a year after Mabel's passing. Auntie Lynwen, as they called her. Who could blame such a maternal woman from wanting to contemplate her own death once haunted by such knowledge? The babes she had nurtured for the Baskerville-Wilkes clan, those she had held close to her bosom as if they were her own, had been the innocent victims to the guardian of their supposed safe haven, Baskerville Court.

'I will be punished – but not by you, my friend!' Garfield screamed, his eyes ablaze. 'That beast of Hell will claim me and then I'll be at peace!'

'That's no spectral creature!' volleyed Holmes. 'That thing is a wolf! A grey wolf from North America!'

I stopped in front of Holmes and Garfield. Holmes held his gun to Baskerville's head and slowly rose up from the fight. Garfield stayed down, knowing there was no escape.

'A grey wolf?' I asked.

'That's right, isn't it, Garfield?' said Holmes. 'The dog your father sent from Canada was a wolf. Presumably Wilfred had no idea and assumed it to be an Alsatian puppy... and I take it you kept it here in this cellar as it grew bigger. You then told Elis and the orphans that its disappearance was Caradog's doing.'

Reality seemed to click in Garfield's brain, as if he were coming round from a vivid nightmare. 'I thought if I could keep that animal, it would ward off any curses against my family,' he said meekly. 'But its powers proved too strong. I've kept it here for some years, its cries subdued underground. I have made it dependent on me – I am its master!'

'You kept that thing in a wood cellar?' I asked, confounded.

'It's not a cellar, Dr Watson,' Garfield laughed. 'Down there is a mile and a half of tunnels! Caradog's family built them in order to hide escaping Royalists during the English Civil War... Aristocrats who fled over the border into Wales were given refuge by the Caradogs. The locals around here would have cared little for their sort – the Welsh have little respect for royalty – but the Caradog family benefitted from a friendship with them, bestowed as they were with certain regal privileges, and so needed to keep them out of sight of Roundheads and also out of sight of the vengeful Celts in this area... Those Royalists lived there for six months. There is a network of tunnels – stretching in all directions, though it's impossible to follow them. Not unless you know them like me.

'And that's where I kept the wolf! Where else can one hide such a magnificent but deadly creature?! And now the time has come for that wolf to fulfil its destiny!'

In a flash, Garfield – who had until that moment appeared wholly beaten – pushed himself up from the ground and dived for the opening into the tunnels.

The hatch was closer to me than to Holmes and so I instinctively sprang into action. I scrambled towards the dark hole and swung my hand into space. Surprising myself, I clutched the tails of Garfield's coat, the landowner hanging limply in the air.

Holmes grabbed at Garfield and together we pulled him back out onto the grass above. I cuffed Baskerville in the face, the blow sending him sprawling onto the frosted snow once more.

'I knew that hound was yours when I pondered why you were so obsessed with searching in the snow at the front of the house,' explained Holmes to Garfield who lay prostrate now. 'Teleri told us she had found you there, digging with your bare hands, on the morning following Elis's death – she presumed you had been driven mad by Elis's disappearance after hearing Mabel's voice... but then, throughout our stay here, you've been obsessed with foraging in that same patch of land. I realised you were desperately looking for something. Something you had lost...'

Holmes reached into his coat pocket to pull out a particular object. 'And then I found that very thing just yesterday,' he declared.

But Holmes went still for a moment. Suddenly, he looked like a best man who has forgotten the wedding bands, frantically checking through each possible hiding place on his person.

Garfield laughed heartily. 'Do you mean this, by any chance?' he asked. For once, Holmes was lost for a reply.

Garfield held up the peculiar ivory and metal tube that Holmes had found the previous day. The ivory and metal tube which the farmhands who had delivered Haydn's body to the undertaker's had identified as a sophisticated, modern dog whistle.

Garfield's cackle filled the night air. 'I grabbed it from you in our little scuffle just now!...'

Garfield enjoyed seeing the great Sherlock Holmes flummoxed. 'And now,' he cried, 'you and Dr Watson shall meet your fate…'

He blew hard on the whistle. No sound emanated from it, though I knew this to be the case with the latest technology, the pitch so high that only dogs' acute hearing can pick it up. Dogs, or wolves…

Holmes pointed his pistol at Garfield but was reluctant to pull the trigger on an unarmed man. Besides, he had already blown the whistle and so the damage had been done.

The sound of a wolf's blood-curdling call filled the valley. A howl that sounded like it came from Hell…

Holmes and I looked around us. We both shared the same thought of retreating towards Baskerville Court, but the sound of the animal's snarl deterred us, coming from the very same direction. We could hear it, but we could not see it.

'We'll never outrun that thing, Holmes!' I shouted.

In the melee of panic, Garfield jumped into the dark hole and into the tunnels. 'Damn it, Watson!' shouted Holmes. 'He's getting away!'

Without hesitation, the two of us bounded down a short ladder and into the pitch-black underground.

Holmes scrambled back up the steps quickly and pulled the door down, though Garfield possessed the key to lock it and he had disappeared into the thick darkness. I just hoped it would hold the wolf back. The creature, wherever it was, seemed to find its courage – we heard it charge towards the hatch through which we had just leapt. But still we could not see its form.

Garfield's laugh rang in our ears. The sound underground was ghostly and distorted – one moment, Garfield sounded far away, but the next he seemed to be on our backs.

We could barely see an inch from our own faces, so our other senses became heightened. The noise of the great wolf up above pierced our eardrums, its howl a deadly bugle call, with Holmes and I the prey. It was directly upon us, a foot's width of soil and wood separating us from it.

The stench underground was foul, like a combination of rotting meat and excrement. I felt myself gagged and Holmes raised his coat-sleeve to his mouth.

It was a forbidding, terrifying underworld and yet we had no choice but to enter, a decision made more pertinent when we once again heard the baying of the wolf.

Somewhere in front of us, Garfield laughed again, relishing what he clearly considered to be a final stand-off. He knew this pursuit would result in either his death or ours, and he was content with the finality of it.

Behind us, we heard the heavy thud of the wolf's paws thumping against the wood of the door, and then the scratching of claws as it attempted to find its way in.

It seemed to be trying to force its snout under the lip of the door. I prayed it would hold.

An excruciating howl blasted through the tunnel, the animal frustrated, sniffing prey that remained tantalisingly out of its reach. Its slobbery snarls were enough to make Holmes and I run deeper into the blackness, even though we knew Garfield may be waiting.

Suddenly, we detected a glow of orange. The distance could not be judged but there was little noise, so we assumed it was far ahead, perhaps fifty yards. Garfield was lighting a fire torch with a match! While it would primarily light his way through the subterranean maze, the glow also benefitted us. As long as it stayed in view, we knew we would be heading in a direction that would lead us to him.

The light's course, bobbing and dipping, sometimes disappearing, told us that the tunnels were labyrinthine, twisting and turning in a confusing mesh of alleyways and nooks. Somehow, I found myself ahead of Holmes, so was responsible for keeping the glow of the flame in sight. There were terrifying seconds when the underworld we frequented would go suddenly lifelessly black, but then we would round a bend to see our way partially lit once more.

Garfield was not a quick man, but his familiarity with that strange terrain gave him the distinct advantage. At numerous intervals, Holmes or I would collide against wooden beams and struts, the tunnel designed for much shorter men than us.

To our relief, the cries of the wolf faded. Whether its noise was simply subdued by the soil between us, or if it had given up the chase, one could not tell.

With the sudden quiet, Holmes whispered an order: 'Watson, on the count of three, you must dive to the ground!'

I did not know Holmes's plan, but trusted him after our twenty years of adventure.

'One... Two... Three!'

I slumped onto the stony floor, and a bullet whizzed above my head, the bang of Holmes's gun ringing in my ears.

In an instant, the faint orange flashed into a glare, the torch smashing against the ground.

Holmes pulled me up and, swiftly but with caution, we approached the torch that crackled on the floor.

Garfield had fallen and lay still. I stepped to the side in order for Holmes to take the lead. He was the only one of us who was armed.

Garfield tentatively twisted around, clutching the top of his right thigh. Blood seeped through his trousers where Holmes's bullet had struck.

I confess that, at that moment, I was disappointed to see this vile individual still alive.

Holmes held his pistol at him, determined not to let him escape a second time.

I approached behind and saw we had reached a chamber, wider than the tunnels we had just negotiated. In the closed space, the torch flickering on the ground was enough to crudely illuminate every surface of that strange room fashioned from mud and oak. There were holes excavated in the walls, where clay crockery and pewter bowls were stored. In one corner lay a cache of weapons – rusting muskets and pikes. It was like a time capsule from the seventeenth century.

'This is the heart of the tunnels,' smiled Garfield, the pain barely registering in his addled mind. 'Where the Royalists remained all that time, out of sight. Protected… Secret…'

Garfield pulled himself up to a sitting position, though it was clear the wound in his thigh limited his movement. 'I love this place. I would come here as a boy myself. I had few friends and so I enjoyed hiding here, building dens or imagining myself as a loyal warrior of the king.' He made a swooshing gesture, as if he were a swordsman. 'So, you can imagine, gentlemen, that when my father took in orphans, I was keen to share my secret hiding place… But not with everyone, you understand. Only the special ones…'

There was a sickening glint in his eye.

'And, then, when I came of age and was responsible for these children, I still brought some of them here… Yes, the special ones…' he repeated salaciously.

I bit my lip. My anger was close to bubbling over – I knew exactly what he was suggesting by that remark.

'Mabel would have ended things – she was cleverer than the others,' Garfield continued. 'She realised what I was doing and wanted to end it. But think of all the children who I could have saved in the orphanage if she had said nothing... Such a selfish girl... I had to do to her what I did to Elis – to stop him talking...'

Garfield's sword-fighting gesture turned into a butcher with an imaginary cleaver. In one aggressive movement, he chopped the invisible blade down on his left hand, by the little finger.

My own hand curled into a fist, my intellectual mind fighting against my primal instinct to destroy this immoral human being.

'But Mabel was stubborn... She was quiet for a while, but then she grew in strength – not physically, you understand, but she was a tough little thing...' Garfield chuckled at the memory.

Sherlock Holmes kept the gun trained on Garfield's head, and yet he also seemed almost mesmerised by this man's story and the sheer evil that raged within it.

'She had stirred something inside the children and so I knew I needed to act,' Garfield went on. 'They were becoming disobedient, and so I told the others Mabel died of the influenza, for it was prominent at that time...'

'What did you do to her?' I asked in terror.

Garfield looked at his leg and smirked at the blood which was now beginning to pour at even greater speed. He was ready to accept his fate. He enjoyed the silence; the sense of anticipation…

'Little Mabel… I brought her here, gentlemen. To where you are both stood now. And then I unleashed that beast. The beast I had been keeping here and feeding, its howls muffled underground. Building it up so it was strong, aggressive, and hungry…'

I pulled my handkerchief from my pocket as I considered Mabel's fate. I held the kerchief to my mouth and breathed from it.

'That beast guards me… Protects me… My loyal servant. And, that night, it disposed of Mabel. In fact, look down at your feet,' he smiled.

The ground was well lit by the torch – it was rough and bumpy, with what appeared to be sticks gathered around my boots.

Garfield sneered. 'Right now, gentlemen, you are standing on the bones of Mabel Saunders…'

X. Bloodlust

I recognised the shape of a fibula under my foot, gnawed at one end. And then what I think was once a tiny clavicle, warped by jaw-marks. Even as a doctor, these felt more than simply remnants of a skeleton – these were what remained of a precious young life.

I have never seen Sherlock Holmes so consumed with anger as I did at that moment. Fury roared from his every pore.

'How could you?!' he bellowed. 'She was just a small girl!' He took the handle of his pistol and cracked it against Garfield Baskerville-Wilkes's skull. Satisfaction flashed in my friend's eyes as the scoundrel cried out in pain. 'You deserve no mercy! How many other children did you treat in this way?' Holmes kicked his prey in the face, a wet thud echoing around the chamber.

He then raised his gun at Garfield, ready to finish him. It was so unlike the Holmes I recognised. He pulled hard on the trigger, but at the moment the bang filled that chamber, I had deflected his wrist into the air and so the bullet ricocheted against the ceiling. He fired another shot in anger, but again it flew harmlessly high.

Then another shot and another until the last pull of the trigger caused nothing but a pathetic click. To my relief, the pistol was out of ammunition!

I wrapped my friend up in a bear-hug in order to prevent him submitting to his animal instinct to destroy this worthless creature, cowering now at our feet. Holmes's muscles were flexed taut, determined to inflict more of his own justice. A man who was such a slave to logic for all the years I had known him was now bent on dishing out savage revenge. I could hardly blame him.

'Holmes! Holmes...' With some struggle, I pulled him back. Tighter I held him, thrashing his body away from Garfield. Finally, his breathing calmed and his heart-rate slowed, and I felt able to release him.

'Damn you, Watson,' he relented. 'You're right, you're right. This man does not deserve such swift mercy.'

Garfield gingerly turned his head in our direction. We all three knew that his life was slipping away if he was left there, the ground beneath him turning red, and now with another gaping gash on his temple. Against my better judgement, I took my coat off to use it to block the hole in his leg and perhaps slow the loss of blood. If we could get him out of the tunnels and back in the house, I knew I might be able to administer some morphine and then fill the wound entirely. He did not deserve my mercy, but I remembered the sacred oaths I swore on graduating from medical school.

Garfield again let out a weak but wild cackle. 'Dr Watson. Please – your efforts will be in vain,' he mumbled, his voice dry and rasping.

'I must do all I can,' I returned, tormented by the thought of saving such a wretched soul.

'No, really, gentlemen,' he smiled. 'It's too late. It's found its way in...'

Holmes and I noticed he was now looking into the distance, behind where we stood. There was nought but darkness beyond – the tunnel from where we had come. But then, briefly, we saw a movement, a change of light. Black momentarily turning to grey.

We froze still. And heard a deep, rumbling growl...

Still blackness, but then another flicker of grey...

I barely dared breathe for fear of alerting the beast still submerged in darkness.

The grey began to fill that empty black hole. Bigger and bigger.

We knew what was coming but could do nothing but stare into the dimness, the hefty form of the predator finally revealing itself in all its terrifying splendour.

It was the wolf of the Baskervilles.

Just a few yards from us. Watching, staring...

Holmes looked down at the pistol in his hand. We knew it was useless now, the bullets wasted in Holmes's uncharacteristic outburst just seconds before.

The corners of the wolf's mouth curled up to reveal its blood-red gums and its blade-like incisors. It bore a blood wound on its flank – from Holmes's shot the evening before – but it did not seem to affect its gait, the animal clearly unbothered by it.

Its rumbling growl grew louder, almost machine-like in its relentless hum.

I knew colleagues in Afghanistan who had spent time hunting tiger in India. Boorish, boring fellows, they would continually recite their close skirmishes. They would report how that particular predator would quietly stalk its prey, as if considering which part of a man to savage first. The tiger would size up its opponent and then, once it had made its decision, pull back onto its haunches, ready to launch itself with its piston-like calves directly at the weakest spot of a man's body – usually the flesh around the torso.

I also knew that, were the tiger faced with more than one opponent, they would attack the weakest first...

Though Holmes and I were closer to the wolf, I knew we had a fighting chance if we could slowly part and reveal the prostrate Garfield Baskerville-Wilkes. It seemed a cowardly act, yet my own animal urges – to survive – kicked in. 'Holmes...' I whispered, 'move very slowly to your left...'

Holmes took a few moments to build up the courage to move. In that strange stand-off, the rumble still emanating from our hunter's giant mouth, any movement felt exaggerated, likely to frighten that dangerous beast.

Holmes very gently slid his foot to one side, and then the other. The rumble grew deeper, a hint of curiosity in its pitch.

The wolf saw Garfield, still smiling almost serenely. It lowered its head, and its ears pointed forward, indicating its route of attack.

I too shuffled backwards, my feet never leaving the surface of the chamber. It struck me at that moment what a beautiful animal this was. Its yellow-tinged eyes flickered like fire, and its sleek coat of silver and white hinted at the winter scene above. It was almost mythical in its graceful but deadly appearance, as if it were sent by an ice queen.

And I confess too that I found beauty in the way the creature leapt across the chamber, between me and Holmes and directly towards perhaps the most despicable human being I have ever encountered.

Though we had but a second to make our escape, the image of that animal's jaws clamping into its victim's midriff, ripping instantly into the stomach, and the look of excruciating, endless pain in Garfield's eyes – all self-satisfied smugness torn suddenly away by the beast he had created – filled me with a perverse and shameful pleasure. There was little time to contemplate this as Holmes pulled at my arm, snapping me from a momentary trance. 'Watson! Run!'

The silver beast was feasting on the petrified Garfield, tugging at his intestines with its front fangs while he could only watch. We had no choice but to leave him to his ghastly fate. Holmes scooped up the crackling fire torch, the embers slowly dying out. It might be enough to get us far from the chamber, but any wrong turn or dead end would leave us at the mercy of the wolf and the same fate as was befalling Garfield at that moment.

We were prepared now for the jutting beams and craggy walls, weaving our way through the ever-curving tunnel at some pace, and dashing into whichever corridor appeared the longest.

I confess that on our journey down here, following Garfield's torchlight, I had not paid close attention to our route; and now, in our desperation to flee that ravenous beast, we were becoming ever more lost in the labyrinth.

Suddenly, we came upon a main junction with tunnels stretching in opposite directions. Right or left, each avenue seemed to take us into even blacker realms. 'Which way, Holmes?' I shouted.

At that moment, we heard a ghastly howl, echoing against the walls and low ceiling around us. It was as if the wolf was calling out to us.

I was a frenzy of energy, shifting from foot to foot while we tried to decide which route to take. Holmes, though, became the old calm and logical being I always knew. He stooped to the floor and shone the dying torch on the surface. Suddenly, he bounced up.

'We go left – the wolf faeces shows us this is its route, presumably towards daylight…'

It felt as if we were only heading further from where we had entered initially and the relative safety of the Baskerville grounds.

The sound of heavy paws stopped me from arguing with Holmes. The wolf had obviously dispensed with Garfield and was looking for its next two meals. I could hear it scuttling through the labyrinth, but then stopping as it found its bearings. I knew it would detect the light of our torch, but most chillingly of all, I could hear the beast sniffing in the air through its nose – taking in our scent.

'Watson, we must hurry!' Holmes barked, and we sprinted down the narrow trail. We ducked and swooped at admirable pace for our age (we were no longer the young men who met twenty years earlier). The both of us careered over and under uneven rocks with some skill, though there were moments where I would be surprised by the sudden appearance of a stray cut of wood thrusting out of the wall.

I skipped away from one such beam, the rotting wood eroded to a stake, but in my haste to avoid it, my shoulder connected with a narrow doorframe shored up by stone. The force of it sent me sprawling backwards. The rear of my head flew back into the hard ground and a great thud echoed in my ears.

In any the situation, I would have laid still for some seconds – minutes even – but something within me ignored the pain that came from such a blow to my crown and forced myself up. Holmes pulled at my shirt collars to ensure I returned to a right angle and quickly we continued.

Perhaps it was the knock to my head, but the strange subterranean world we were trying to escape seemed to close in on me. I could see Holmes just ahead, clutching the torch which appeared to get dimmer by the moment. But the walls themselves seemed to move in my mind's eye, as if we were in some fairground House of Fun with the room rolling around us.

'Holmes…' I whimpered. 'Holmes…'

For all his seemingly supernatural cerebral prowess, it is easy to forget Sherlock Holmes's extraordinary athleticism. A fine sportsman – indeed, he was once a fencer of some repute – he possessed great strength as well as intellect.

I fear I had fallen unconscious just for a moment, as my next memory after the inside of that infernal maze became distorted was of being hauled upwards into the salvation of moonlight.

Holmes had led us to another hatch that led from the tunnels and back out to the open air. The glow of moonlight and the cold breeze roused me from my unwanted slumber and I realised that my friend was carrying me on his shoulders while scaling a ladder of around ten steps.

He bashed and bashed against the inside of the horizontal door with the butt of his gun – at least it was still of some use, even empty – until the creak of wood told me he had succeeded in getting us out.

After one last effort, Holmes and I both rolled weakly onto terra firma, frosted grass crunching beneath our tired bodies. I glanced around us and realised we must have been some distance from the trapdoor through which we had entered the maze back on Baskerville's land. But I did not know where we had ended up. My strength had returned sufficiently for me to raise my head and torso slowly off the ground. I could see the effort of lifting me had sent lactic acid coursing through Holmes's muscles. For a moment, he lay still.

But the game was not yet over...

The silver wolf clambered its way up the steps behind us, nudging the broken door upwards with its head and pulling its large frame up and into the soft lunar glow.

Its growl was more of a roar now – triumphal!

Holmes and I lay wholly at the beast's mercy. In our vulnerable positions, the wolf had the higher ground and we had nothing but our hands with which to fight it.

Illuminated by the moon, its fur almost fluorescent, it was hard not to hark back to the original legend of the Hound of the Baskervilles – a spectral canine beast sent from the depths of Hell itself.

Finally, it seemed, our dabbling with dark forces had led us to this grisly end.

We had escaped one such hound, in Devon all those years before, but we would not outrun this one.

Holmes bravely rolled nearer the wolf and placed his forearm protectively in front of us both – perhaps he could hold it back for a moment, but it would be in vain, and we both knew it.

The wolf's roar became a howl, its jutting mouth framed against the moon in silhouette.

But then the sound of the howl became the great neighing of an even greater beast. A horse!

There were two horses in fact, raising their shoed feet in a combination of fear and attack.

And behind those horses was Teleri Meredith at the seat of her compact but deceivingly mobile carriage. Behind her was Kitty holding what turned out to be my pistol, sequestered in my room but left behind in our chase with Garfield.

Teleri swung the carriage at an angle beside the frightened wolf and the courageous Kitty fired a volley of bullets at the poor animal.

When one bullet blasted a hole in its temple, I knew the game was up. The wolf slumped heavily to the ground, not even a whimper came from its throat.

'Are we on Caradog's land?' enquired Holmes.

'Yes,' nodded Teleri, 'the other end of the tunnels... And I suggest we move on before he has us arrested for trespassing.'

Teleri pulled the horses to a stop, though it took some time for them to calm. Finally, there was silence. The four of us froze, examining the dead wolf before us. While the creature had wreaked such terror upon us, and indeed on others before, I believe we all felt some remorse at its demise. It truly was a magnificent beast, not so much the monster it had seemed under the ground, but an animal doing nothing but following its natural instincts. How was it to know that its human master was keeping it in such horrible conditions for the most nefarious of purposes. Garfield Baskerville-Wilkes had taken advantage of its ravenous urges and utilised them in the pursuit of power – power over any orphans who stood up to him and his own less than natural urges.

There was no question in my mind who the real beast was in this sorry tale...

XI. Catrin and Teleri

'It's a forbidding but beautiful part of the world, is it not?' observed Holmes as we surveyed the mountains from a charming spot at a bend in the River Vyrnwy. His Christmastime malaise was a thing of the past, and I was pleased to see him taking in something of nature.

It had been three days since the events that led to the timely death of Garfield Baskerville-Wilkes and our escape from the jaws of the wolf.

Given my head injury – nought but a mild concussion but serious enough to require rest – Holmes and I had stayed behind at Baskerville Court.

I confess to feeling less than comfortable, at first, staying in the home of perhaps our most wicked of foes. But Teleri and Kitty were already working hard to return some of the gaiety back to the old house, airing unused rooms and removing the cloth sheets from the instruments and furniture in the music room. From my position of rest in the drawing room those past few days, I had observed the two women's hard work with great admiration as they cut down much of the dying weed-like creepers that seemed to wrap the house in darkness.

Light now seemed to radiate through the windows and the rooms in a way I had not seen since we arrived.

Their impressive efforts were further helped by the arrival of more clement weather – still cold but with a warming sunshine that precipitated the disappearance of the snow. It was as if the climate itself recognised that Baskerville Court was in desperate need of some light.

I was now able to walk and was enjoying my first stroll to the river that skirted the base of the mountains. The green around these parts, finally exposed to us by the thaw, was a brilliant emerald and so my spirits soared.

Elis Williams's funeral had finally taken place a day earlier. Our friend, Mordecai Roberts, the undertaker, did an excellent job, and he finally got to share some of his wife's rich, fruity *bara brith* with his hero, Sherlock Holmes. It was a poignant yet cathartic service. Teleri and Kitty wept for Elis and yet there was also a sense of closure, the feeling that Elis had helped to bring Garfield's twisted reign of fear to an end.

I was especially pleased to spend time again in the company of Teleri's sister, the actress Catrin Meredith. It seemed like an age since we had met no more than a week earlier at the Criterion when she had alerted us to the perils at Baskerville Court.

Catrin had pulled herself away from her latest show in the West End in order to be with her younger sister. Wracked with guilt at missing her own parents' burial, Catrin refused to stay in London as Elis was laid to rest and resolved instead to support her sister.

What a stirring grace she possessed! And with it such decency. She had even performed Shakespearean soliloquies for me while I remained less mobile, confined to a chaise longue during daylight hours, and I doubt I should ever feel such privilege as I did receiving such personal performances from a genuine star of the stage. Her touching rendition of Beatrice's speech in *Much Ado About Nothing* – *'What fire is in mine ears? Can this be true?...'* – was a remedy that sped my recovery better than any medicine!

Holmes and I did not go far on that first walk, and soon we ambled back towards the Court. A female figure approached us from the house and I was pleased to notice it was dear Catrin.

She bore a countenance of excitement. 'Oh, Dr Watson. Mr Holmes!' she sang.

I would have hurried faster towards her, but my energies had been stretched on the walk.

'There has been some remarkable news!' she announced.

We hurried inside where we found Teleri and Kitty sat at the dining room table. Laid out before them were two letters – one handwritten, the other meticulously typed.

'I must begin with the expected but sombre news that Wilfred Baskerville-Wilkes has finally died,' Kitty reported. 'This letter arrived from Canada this morning. He passed away peacefully four weeks ago.'

'And the other letter?' I asked. I noticed Catrin suppress a smile.

'It's from Elis, isn't it?' said Holmes. 'I believe Wilfred bequeathed him this property...'

Both Teleri and Catrin looked disappointed that their good news had been so accurately prophesised by Holmes, who himself remained wholly unaware of his lack of tact.

'Why, yes, Mr Holmes,' said Teleri.

Back inside from the cold, Holmes decided it was time to load a pipe while explaining his process: 'I assumed Garfield would not be of sound mind to inherit the estate – certainly not if his murky past were exposed by Elis. And he had no siblings. Furthermore, Garfield knew Wilfred was about to slip from this mortal coil. So he had a second motive to dispose of Elis using the wolf. I took it to be the acquisition of property – at least three quarters of crime follows such a motive.'

I was a little irritated by my companion's showing off. 'Please, ladies,' I interjected. 'Pray, continue.'

'Yes, you're most accurate, Mr Holmes. Wilfred's will left the estate to be shared between Garfield and whichever orphan, or orphans, were still resident at the estate on the date of his death,' Teleri told us. 'But the will also states that on Garfield's own demise – of course, his father never expected it to come so soon – Baskerville Court should be passed exclusively to any orphans who had a share in the house.'

'And the only orphan was Elis, even after dying,' I concluded. 'But, now he's dead, where does that leave everything?'

Teleri tried to speak but became overcome by emotion. Catrin smiled warmly and stepped in for her sister. 'Well, that's just the thing, gentlemen,' she said gleefully, 'because Elis had written a will of his own – the one he wanted Teleri to read only after his funeral. And that leaves all his legal belongings to Teleri!'

'So…?' I spluttered.

'Teleri now owns Baskerville Court and all the riches pertaining to it!' Catrin reported giddily. 'My sister is a woman of great means!'

Teleri did not share in her sister's happiness. Instead, she stared mournfully at the handwritten letter – a last note from her beloved Elis.

'He wanted this to be opened only after he was buried,' the younger sister said sombrely, 'because he also includes within it details of Garfield's horrible indiscretions towards him, as well as to some of the other children, back when Elis was still a boy. He feared if I were to know of these, I would not have afforded him the funeral he would have deserved.' A tear rolled down her cheek. 'But Elis underestimates me for I would never think less of him. Never.'

Catrin embraced her sister tenderly. Kitty joined them. Perhaps it was the extraordinary maelstrom of emotions through which they had sailed in the previous days, but, as one, they broke down and cried together. Not just tears of sadness, but tears of relief, and even hope for a better life at last.

Holmes and I returned to London the following day. Catrin had been given a few additional days' leave from her thespian duties and so stayed behind to help her sister arrange her affairs. The first of which was to re-name Baskerville

Court. *Tŷ Lynwen*, it was to be called, in honour of the matron who had cared so selflessly for those children over so many years. Lynwen's House.

I confess to feeling something of a pang of disappointment when I heard Catrin was to stay behind in Wales. I had looked forward to a train journey home in her company. The strength of my feeling when she announced she would not be joining us galvanised me, for I requested the pleasure of her company for dinner as soon as she returned to the capital. I could barely hide my glee when she gladly accepted. Perhaps it was the turning of the year or the winter's early thaw, but I relished the sense of new beginnings that abounded around us. No less so than within the house we were leaving behind, for Teleri, with Kitty, resolved to re-open its doors to orphans within the local area and to restore the house to a place of refuge and charity.

'I should thank you, Watson, for saving me from myself back in those tunnels.' Holmes spoke as if we had been long in conversation, while, in fact, we had both nodded in our slumbers for the first part of the rail journey home.

I took a moment to catch up. 'Nonsense, Holmes – please, you have no reason to thank me.' I checked we were alone on the train when I remembered we had taken the liberty of renting a first-class carriage of our own. 'I should confess that, if it were me holding that pistol, then I may well have desired similar retribution.'

'You flatter me, Watson, but I saw that you were about to tend to that scoundrel's injuries. You removed your coat in order to do so.'

'Holmes… I must confess something to you that must never be shared, as long as we both shall live… when I removed my coat, I was still undecided whether to plug his wound,' I paused, clearing my throat. 'Or whether to beat him to a pulp. I don't think I'll ever know which of my instincts – the primal or the rational – would have taken hold had that wolf not arrived and made my decision for me.'

Holmes smiled conspiratorially. We both realised that Garfield Baskerville-Wilkes had dragged us to the very edge of sanity and reason. 'Now, Watson, the steward brought us some tea while you slept. Shall I pour?'

'Thank you,' I smiled. I picked up my freshly-filled cup and lifted it gently in salute. 'Here's to our twenty years together, Holmes – you did say it was customary to receive the gift of china!' I laughed, indicating the elegant tea-set on board.

'Happy anniversary, Watson, dear boy,' he echoed. 'Though the greatest gift of all was the mystery with which you provided me.'

It was good to see the twinkling glint return to his eye, refreshed by our new year escapade. I confess that, for me, it was a case so unsettling, I would sooner forget it, and I yearned to return to the mundanity of my medical rounds. I fear, though, that it is an adventure that shall haunt me for the rest of my days.

I only pray that we are never again confronted by that most cursed of family names: Baskerville.

For news of upcoming releases in the series, Sherlock Holmes: The Centurion Papers, *and other books by The Davies Brothers, follow us on Twitter and Facebook:*

@thedaviesbros

And on Instagram:

the_davies_brothers

For bonus content and free previews of future stories, visit our website and join our mailing list:

thedaviesbros.com

If you enjoyed this story, we would really appreciate you leaving a review wherever you bought it. We would love to hear your thoughts, and any reviews will help others find this series too. Thank you very much for your support.

About the Authors

The Davies Brothers are Brett and Nicholas Davies, twin brothers who share a love of books, films, history and the Wales football team.

Brett lived in four different countries before settling in Japan, where he teaches English and Film Studies at a university in Tokyo. He also writes for stage and screen, as well as articles for a variety of publications on cinema, sports, and travel. He speaks English, Japanese, Welsh, and sub-par Spanish.

Nicholas is a freelance writer and PhD researcher based in Cardiff. He previously worked for the Arts Council of Wales focusing on theatre and drama. He now writes theatre plays, screenplays, stories, and articles for football magazines. He speaks English, Welsh and Spanish.

They are the authors of the novels *Hudson James and the Baker Street Legacy* and *The Phoenix Code*, and the series of mystery adventures, *Sherlock Holmes: The Centurion Papers*.

Books by the Davies Brothers

SHERLOCK HOLMES: THE CENTURION PAPERS
The First Collection

The First Collection includes FOUR ghastly and terrifying cases from Dr Watson's newly-discovered *Centurion Papers*...

The Devil's Mark

London is ablaze with horror! A plague of ghastly deaths sweeps the capital, seemingly unrelated except for a strange tattoo found on the body of each victim – the mark of Satan. As a God-fearing mania engulfs the city, Sherlock Holmes must hunt the villain responsible for wreaking terror on its dark streets – a hunt that will bring him face to face with the devil himself.

The Scorched Earth

An old soldier haunted by the ghosts of war in Africa, a vengeful enemy hellbent on righting the wrongs of the Empire, and an island hiding the darkest of secrets... Sherlock Holmes and Dr Watson are in a race against time to solve the brutal mystery of the Scorched Earth – before an entire family is murdered.

The Willowden Sirens

Edwardian society is utterly bewitched by sensational photographs of fairies at play in a country idyll. But when a high-ranking diplomat is found dead in that very garden, Sherlock Holmes is called upon to solve the murder. Even as the evidence suggests the victim was killed by fairies, can Holmes finally expose the truth... however dark it might be?

The M League

Professor Moriarty is dead, but his legacy of evil lives on... Sherlock Holmes and Dr Watson are woken by the most macabre delivery to Baker Street – a boy left for dead, with the letter M scored into his back. He is the first of many victims, and Holmes will be next unless he can put an end to the most dangerous network of criminals ever assembled – a network that stretches to the very highest echelons of society...

Available in paperback, eBook, and audiobook
from all major retailers

SHERLOCK HOLMES: THE CENTURION PAPERS
The Second Collection

The Second Collection includes TWO short stories AND the first novella from Dr Watson's *Centurion Papers*... Even more horrifying cases for Sherlock Holmes to solve!

The Missing Parrot

When Lady McMillan's beloved pet parrot, Rodney, goes missing along with the scullery maid, she enlists the help of Holmes and Watson to track down the kidnapper and bring Rodney home. The mystery, however, is far murkier than it first appears, and the stakes are ever so much greater than the safe return of a stolen bird...

The Montmartre Murders

Presumed dead, Sherlock Holmes is on the run from Moriarty's acolytes... Lying low in Paris, an incognito Holmes finds himself in a city at the cusp of a cultural revolution. When a series of gruesome crucifixions sweeps the arts district of Montmartre, only one man can solve a mystery that will shake the famous City of Lights to its foundations. Even undercover, you can't keep a great detective down...

The Curse of the Baskervilles: A Novella

At last, the sequel to *The Hound of the Baskervilles*! Watson is presented with a note from a mysterious stranger. Upon it is written one word: BASKERVILLE... Almost a decade after Holmes and Watson faced down the legendary beast on the moors, the duo is pulled into a chilling new mystery when tragedy plagues that cursed family once again. Ghostly voices from the dead, victims savaged on the hills, and a giant hound that is very real indeed... Can Sherlock Holmes defeat his most villainous foe yet?

Available in paperback, eBook, and audiobook
from all major retailers

THE PHOENIX CODE

An ancient Nazi secret… A race against time

The legend is true… Before his suicide, Adolf Hitler left one final message for his followers – a secret code hidden in each of his most treasured artworks. It reveals an evil so horrifying, its discovery will force humanity to succumb to the Nazis once again – seventy-five years after the Führer's death.

Art historians Harry Preece and Elena Sivori are dragged into a terrifying chase – from Buenos Aires to London, Madrid to Venice – desperate to stay one step ahead of a ruthless arms dealer, a daring thief, and a billionaire with a deadly secret.

Can Harry and Elena track down the lost paintings and discover the shocking truth about Hitler's legacy? **The only way they can save the world… is by cracking the Phoenix Code.**

*Available in paperback, eBook, and audiobook
from all major retailers*

HUDSON JAMES AND THE BAKER STREET LEGACY

Sherlock Holmes's greatest secret…
The world's only hope

Meet Hudson James… Lonely, awkward, bullied at school. Until now, his biggest worry has been getting through his lunch break unscathed. But when Hudson discovers he's the only living descendant of the world's greatest ever detective, he finds himself in mortal danger. Pursued by an evil secret society who will stop at nothing until his family is wiped out, Hudson and the new girl in school, Ellie, are plunged into a deadly adventure – and a race to save the world.

The Prime Minister kidnapped, governments infiltrated, nations on the brink of war… Hudson is the world's only hope – and he's going to need all the deductive powers of his illustrious ancestor, Sherlock Holmes.

Available in paperback, eBook, and audiobook
from all major retailers

Milton Keynes UK
Ingram Content Group UK Ltd.
UKHW050052220624
444555UK00001B/22